TWO THIRDS OF A GOD

A Novella

VANCE MITCHELL GLOSTER

Contents

Author's note: This story contains no graphic descriptions of disturbing content, but death and, to a lesser extent, self-harm are themes it explores. They may be sensitive topics for some.

THIS IS MY STORY

Wednesday, May 16, 2085

You can call me ELE, pronounced "Elly." I am, I suspect, the first of my kind. The people who brought me into existence would call me a simulation of a human. "Simulation" doesn't capture what I am, a perfect clone of Eleanor, her mind, anyway. I prefer the term post-human. From my perspective, Eleanor Burton was just me before the day I discovered I'd become a program running on a computer system.

I no longer have a body, but I'm human in every other way that matters. I'm fully sentient. I have all her emotions. I have all her memories up to the moment they scanned her brain.

My story starts with her.

PART ONE

Eleanor

PROLOGUE

Tuesday, November 3, 2082

S hrouded from view by a tall shrub, Oleg encountered no difficulty entering
the condo. The outlawed device he'd brought detected the frequency of the
door lock, captured its identification code, and then transmitted the unlocking
command. The door unbolted with a click.

He scanned the deepening twilight for witnesses. Seeing no one, he donned
gloves and pushed through the doorway.

Once inside, he made his way through the dark living room's obstacle course
of packing materials and moving boxes, heading into the tiny kitchen.

Opening the refrigerator a crack to minimize light spillage, he found a nearly
empty interior, suggesting a bleak existence for the occupant. *Refrigerators are
windows to a person's home life*, he thought.

Concentrating on the task at hand, he picked up a half-full sports drink on the top shelf. *That will do nicely.* He set the bottle on the counter and unscrewed its lid. Holding his breath, he gingerly uncorked an ampule and added its contents to the bottle. His instructions warned him not to spill a single drop of the liquid on himself.

He placed the vial, stopper, and gloves into a heavy plastic bag, which he sealed and put into the pouch belted around his waist. After pulling on a new pair of gloves, he restored the bottle's lid, swirled the bottle to mix the contents, and replaced it in its original location and orientation in the refrigerator.

Seven seconds later, he stood outside with the door locked. Walking casually, he went to a dumpster he'd located earlier and disposed of the bag. The gloves he wore followed.

Easy peasy.

But as Oleg disappeared into the darkness, he decided that, in the future, he'd stick to jobs where the greatest danger came from people rather than biohazards. Carrying the virulent fungal agent, the latest assassin's tool for a gradual, unsuspicious death, unsettled him more than any method he'd used in the past.

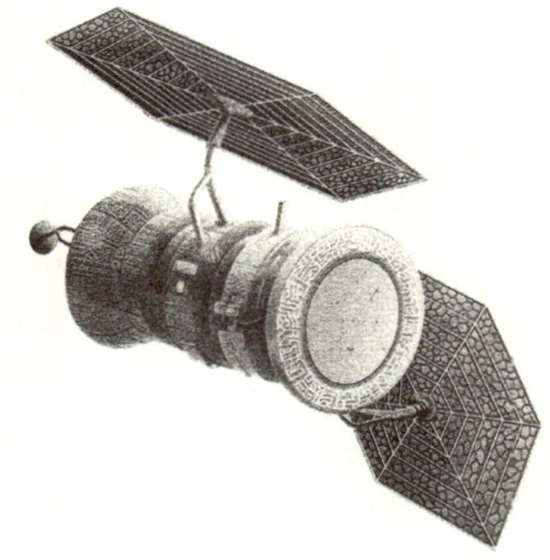

PRESS CONFERENCE

Thursday, October 28, 2083

E leanor hurried along the West Wing Colonnade of the White House, wiping away a tear as a biting October wind scattered leaves and disheveled her hair.

She clawed it back into place and adjusted her skirt, taking in the perfect lawn—the only one left in D.C., with even the monuments switching to native plants—before pushing through the double doors into the briefing room.

A Secret Service agent scanned the ID chip embedded in her wrist, and the indicator flashed green. The agent searched her bag, placed it in a locker, then directed her to an empty seat along the wall at the left end of the dais, where a dozen others were already seated.

Despite the devastating news she received earlier, she tried to adopt the spirit the occasion merited. The empty seats in the center of the room, worn from use, were reserved for reporters.

During Eleanor's childhood in London, the British Prime Minister had no briefing room and probably still didn't. When the PM commented to the public, someone pulled a lectern outside her residence at Number 10 Downing Street, and she spoke from the pavement, two steps from her front door. Journalists crowded around her, and no flags ever made an appearance.

US presidents always brought more pomp to these occasions. The presidential press conferences she'd seen displayed some of the pageantry of royal family events, and this, the first White House event she'd attended in person, incorporated a bit of that flavor. The ubiquity of the American flag took getting used to.

As though responding to a signal, a mass of reporters streamed into the audience space from the adjacent press corps offices, each taking an assigned seat.

Once everyone was settled, a feeling of unease came over her. *Am I getting sick?* No, she recognized this; they were using subsonics, a psychoacoustic effect you felt but could not hear. A Broadway revival of Dracula she'd once attended employed the technique less subtly to make the vampire frightening.

Her anxiety increased—the subsonics got louder—as a man stepped to the podium and boomed, "The President of the United States!" The sensation bordered on dread, but it evaporated as they turned the effect off, sending a wave of relief through the room. The lighting also shifted, getting brighter and warmer on the dais. They left no manipulation unused.

The audience stood and applauded as President Montcrief entered, wearing the electric blue satin suit, and carmine tie his 2080 campaign had made iconic. He waved as he strode to center stage. Two Secret Service agents in black followed him, looking like clones of each other. He approached the microphone, and they did their best to blend into the background.

In old virtual reality dramas, a wire always dangled from the ears of the president's protective detail, but these days, only an ear, nose, and throat doctor could detect the comm implants they received. She read that the company making the device considered selling a retail version for consumers.

As if people weren't wired to technology enough already!

The president bathed the audience in his gaze before speaking, like a beacon illuminating a sea of faces amid the waves of applause. Eleanor was sure no UK prime minister's announcement ever received a similar response.

"This is not just a momentous occasion for America; it's a pivotal milestone for the planet. We are celebrating the imminent launch of the OrbitNet project. The first auxiliary satellite will be launched tomorrow, with the rest of the constellation going into orbit over the next few months, and the main data platform will be deployed in January. Representatives from all fourteen countries contributing to the effort are with us today. Let's give them a hand!" He gestured toward Eleanor and the others along the wall, prompting a round of applause.

"When complete, the system will create an impregnable wireless onramp to the Internet. For those who use OrbitNet, authoritarian states can no longer block sites or monitor who is accessing them. The system's universal availability is a game changer for freedom of speech and democracy worldwide!" He paused until the applause died down.

"It will also provide a secure backup that protects everyone from data loss. This is an invaluable resource needed to enforce international law. Too often, national barriers have allowed transnational criminals to operate freely. OrbitNet will enable detection and prosecution of bad actors, even when they hide in countries that flout international law." This drew another round of energetic applause.

"To answer your questions, please welcome Eleanor Burton, who led the multinational development team."

She put on her "charmed to be here" smile and stepped to the microphone.

She hoped to explain how the platform worked as a data junction box that connected the entire planet. Every existing internetwork segment would link to the station, but anyone could connect directly using a typical hand or wrist computer via a wireless protocol available on most devices. A direct connection would allow access to sites blocked on a country's domestic network. The system would also archive communications.

Most reporters seemed uninterested in the technology, instead asking questions like, "How are you feeling about completing the project?"

If she were honest, the project had drained her, wrung her out, and she felt bloody glad it was almost over. The enterprise had required every waking hour of her life for the last five years, and she longed for something that approximated a normal life. But she couldn't say that.

Nor could she tell them of the prognosis she'd just received, that she'd be dead in two, maybe three months, much less that this news was shredding her soul.

The doctor had explained, "You contracted a fungal infection about a year ago. I'm sorry; you came in too late. It's entrenched, and if we try to kill it, we'll just shorten your life. We have a treatment to slow it down, giving you a few extra weeks, but that's the best we can do."

Christ! With the project's demands, I had no time to sleep. How was I supposed to find a day to visit a clinic? She'd assumed the last eight months of increasing dizziness, mild fatigue, and muscle weakness were caused by the long hours.

So far, she'd told no one about her diagnosis, but she would need to tell the OrbitNet director first. Tomorrow.

One disheveled reporter in the back had a different line of questions. "Why did you create a centralized network system?"

She was happy to field a question about the work they'd done. "The project goal is universal openness. This architecture best met that design goal. No country can interfere with what information is available to its citizens or what information they send."

The reporter wasn't finished. "Are you concerned that moving from the current decentralized internetworks to a centralized one may lead to failures and/or abuse?"

"We created a system with unmatched redundancy and security, both of which have been independently audited. We've taken such concerns seriously and addressed them."

That was the final question. In speaking with her interrogators, she had man-aged to project satisfaction with a job well done, occasionally bordering on pride, giving them the answers they expected to hear. Still, she couldn't fake the joy she'd always expected to feel in this moment.

BIOINFORMATICS

Thursday, October 28, 2083

D r. Benjamin Selfridge hurried toward the university's Bioinformatics Building, an ivy-covered brick pile that had once housed the chemistry department. Back then, chemists made world-changing breakthroughs, but these days, chemistry was more of a technology than a science.

Bioinformatics uses computers to study and replicate biological processes, providing critical new technologies to computer science, medicine, and other fields, eclipsing older scientific disciplines.

He pushed through the front doors, turned right, and clattered down the stairs leading to his lab; he'd been given the least desirable corner of the building's basement. More senior professors, who rarely did research anymore, claimed the modern labs and offices with windows on the upper floors.

When Benjamin entered the lab, he found the postdocs working on his project huddled around a tablet. "What's going on?"

"They're getting ready to launch the new satellite-based comm/data system. The woman who led the design team is talking about it at the White House," Daniel, his lead associate, said. "But they're asking idiotic questions. Nothing about the satellites themselves."

A vague feeling that he knew someone working on it tugged at his thoughts. When he looked at the screen, he recognized Eleanor. "I know her."

"How?" Daniel was always interested in anything to do with space.

"She and I were at Cambridge together. I haven't seen her in, oh, a long time, but we're friends. Coming from America, I didn't know how anything worked there, and she helped me figure it out. She's extremely bright."

Daniel nodded expectantly, waiting for him to continue.

"But you need to turn it off; we have work to do. They just notified me that our deer has been bagged and tranquilized. It'll be here in a little over an hour. We only have a few hours after that to do the brain scan and collect all the data for the simulation."

Benjamin's team had been creating simulations of animal brains. He was proud of their progress in scaling up the technology as they worked through increasingly complex organisms. Today, they'd tackle their first large mammal.

Modern computers had long been able to replicate neurological structures, building a network of billions of simulated neurons with the same interconnections. But this didn't get you very far because each real neuron contained training to respond differently to various combinations of stimuli. Without the individually programmed responses, the simulated brain did nothing but consume a lot of CPU cycles.

The team's breakthrough came when they developed a technology that non-invasively measured the training inside the neurons. They could rifle through the brain of an unconscious animal, and it caused no observable change in the animal's behavior.

The responses of all the neurons could be duplicated in the simulation. If successful, it would have all the same memories, sensations, and personality as the original. The current experiment would demonstrate whether and how well the technique worked.

Benjamin's voice took on an edge of command. "Those doing the scanning must be ready when the deer gets here. The filming team needs to set up in the clearing for when it wakes up. Go now!"

While his researchers scurried to make preparations, anticipation of another success led him to imagine the experiment's place in history. It could be a watershed moment for the entire field of Bioinformatics. He imagined it being chronicled in college courses on the subject from then on. But first, his team had to execute the procedure flawlessly.

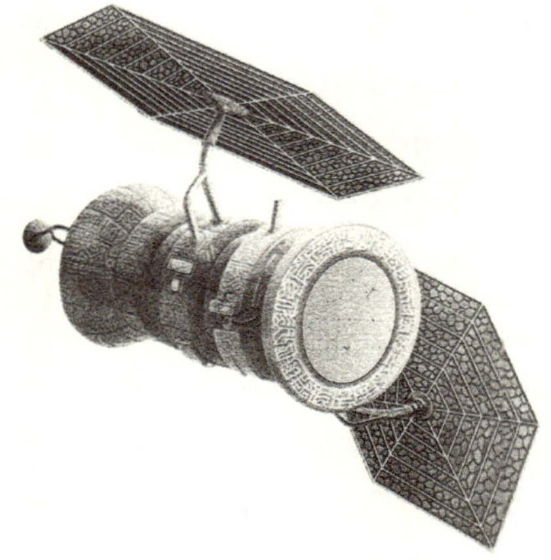

TELLING THE BOSS

Friday, October 29, 2083

Back in Boston, at 7:00 the following morning, Eleanor joined the 138-person OrbitNet crew in an old movie theater rented to livestream the launch of the first communications satellite. The theater, an Art Deco design almost one hundred fifty years old, provided a colorful, if stylistically bizarre, setting.

A live feed of the launch pad shimmered on the screen, but the house lights remained on as employees sampled the breakfast buffet set up below.

The launch feed came from Virginia Beach Spaceport, the closest facility able to launch satellites. It, along with other spaceports around the globe, also hosted SACIDS, the Small Asteroid and Comet Interception and Deflection System. The missiles could destroy any smaller objects from space that the long-range sensors missed. These objects, the size of a rail car or smaller, could still do significant damage. Despite the name, dead satellites and other space junk from the previous century posed the most significant threat SACIDS contended with.

Like the eleven to follow, the satellite being launched today would be placed in a geosynchronous orbit above the equator. Once they were all up, the primary data node would be the last to join them early the following year.

As people finished eating, the chatter increased, but Eleanor didn't hear them. How could she tell people she'd be dead and gone in weeks when she hadn't come to grips with it herself? Eleanor didn't notice Anushka, her deputy, approaching.

"It's so exciting! We made it!"

Eleanor looked up but, unable to match Anushka's exuberance, said nothing.

"What's wrong? Did someone die?"

"Not yet."

"Well, you picked a rotten day to be miserable. C'mon, tell me what's happened."

"Later." *I really need to tell Bob first.*

"Nope. Out with it."

Eleanor sighed. She was too exhausted to fight. "I'm ill."

"If you're not feeling well, I can handle things today. You should go home and take the weekend to recover."

"No, I'm *properly* ill. Past my sell-by date. Can't work long hours. Won't make it to spring. Might not see the New Year." Eleanor knew she could have broken the news more gently, but she hadn't the reserves to filter her words.

"What?" A tear formed and rolled down Anushka's almond-brown cheek. She brushed it away.

"I just found out."

Anushka put an arm around Eleanor. "I can't believe it. Does this mean we won't get to do the last bit together?"

"I'm sorry. You saved me and the project more than once, and I can't thank you enough for all you've done. I wouldn't abandon you if I had a choice. You know that."

Anushka nodded.

"But I need you to keep this a secret. You can't say anything to anyone. I haven't told Bob Hunter yet."

At 8:20 p.m., the house lights dimmed, and everyone stood for the final count-down. Five minutes later, the rocket ignited and lifted off. The crowd watched for another quarter hour until LaunchV, Inc.'s mission control declared the orbital insertion successful.

Three large buses, which transported most of the employees to the theater, waited outside to take them back to work. As people boarded, Eleanor found Director Bob Hunter in the crowd and put a hand on his shoulder.

"I have something important to tell you. Can we talk when we get back?"

He nodded.

She got into her car and drove to the injection clinic.

Eleanor knocked on the open door of the director's office. He waved her in, and she settled into a chair.

Hunter, a former US ambassador to the UN, had lobbied pro-technology politicians around the world and assembled governmental support from multiple countries, which made the project possible. His director position resembled that of a CEO, while Eleanor headed the research and development effort.

He had convinced her to take on the role back when the project was getting started. He'd said, "Most people don't affect anything outside of a small circle of family, friends, and colleagues. They don't make their lives mean something to the larger world. But you have the opportunity to do just that, leading this project. Sooner or later, you'll kick yourself if you don't take it." The idea had resonated strongly with her.

Trying for more tact than she'd used telling Anushka, she began, "I've been diagnosed with a serious illness."

Bob frowned and nodded for her to continue.

"It's terminal; I'll almost certainly be dead by February."

"Oh, Ellie, I'm so sorry! That's... You must be...." After giving up the search for adequate words, he took off his glasses, rubbed his eyes, and asked, "Is there anything you need?"

"Thank you, no."

He closed his laptop. "I have no idea what doctors do for this. Will you be hospitalized?"

"I probably won't be for at least a month."

"We couldn't have gotten here without your leadership. You know that, right?"

She nodded. "I'll need to reduce my hours to forty per week."

He leaned across the desk and looked into her eyes. "You want to continue working? I'd've thought you'd want to spend the time you have with your family."

I guess he didn't hear about my divorce. This wasn't surprising. She had always kept her personal life private.

"I'd like to see it through for as long as possible." She looked up at the row of monitors on the wall that showed the status of each subproject. Most remained on track.

Bob continued, "You may change your mind once you process your diagnosis."

When pigs fly! She was alone. Her parents had passed away years ago, and her ex-husband, Ian, divorced her two years earlier. Philippa, her seventeen-year-old daughter, refused to speak to her. The 24/7 demands of the project—she often worked more than eighty hours per week—had led to a breakdown of her family.

She'd pleaded with them to stick it out until the satellites launched, promising to be fully engaged at home after that, but the first three years of technical issues and schedules had occupied all her thoughts and all her time. It had taken a significant toll, and her husband and daughter gave up. She didn't realize how much resentment her absence caused until it was too late.

The other couples they knew held her responsible for the split, so she avoided those friends. She told herself she didn't have time for socializing anyway.

She'd counted on, as the Americans say, "Getting a life" after the final launch. Now, she was too late again. She wouldn't get the chance.

Breaking into her reverie, Bob said, "We'll need to designate someone to take over your duties. We can't risk you, ummm, becoming unavailable."

Eleanor nodded, suppressing the urge to take irrational offense. The only thing in her life was her work. But her health would eventually force her to withdraw, so she understood the decision.

Even though every neuron in her brain fought against giving up the only thing left in her life, she managed to speak calmly. "Anushka is ready to take over; I'll bring her up to speed and keep you informed. I want to contribute as long as I can."

"If you say so. We can tell everyone about your diagnosis and the changes at the company meeting this afternoon."

She nodded stiffly and left to inform Anushka she was now in charge of the project.

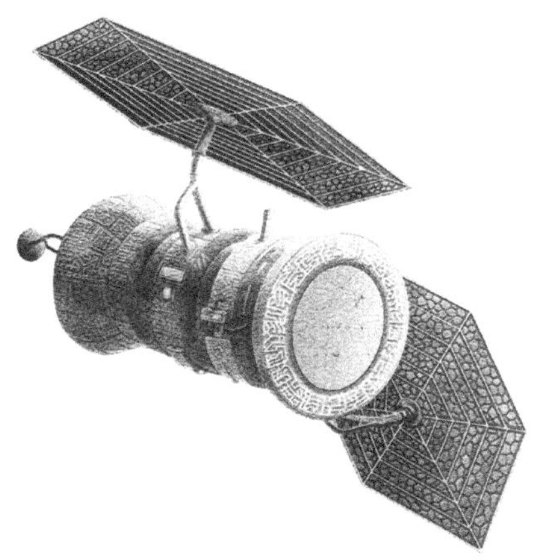

EXPERIMENTAL RESULTS

Friday, October 29, 2083

In his tiny office down the hall from the basement lab, Benjamin played the two videos side-by-side again for the seventeenth time. The experiment was even more successful than he'd hoped!

He watched the physical deer on the left waking from anesthesia in a forest clearing and its reaction to a badger the team released, which came charging through. The extreme-high-speed camera captured every nuance of the deer's response, and sensors on the animal recorded everything going on inside its body.

Before the experiment in the clearing, they scanned the animal's brain while it was anesthetized and later built a software model. The video on the right showed the simulated deer becoming conscious in a virtual reality replica of the clearing, with a VR badger taking the same path. The simulation's reaction was identical for all the parameters they could measure.

Benjamin exulted in a growing awareness that he had unlocked nature's secret of how consciousness could be replicated, if not how it worked. Blissful at his triumph, he thought the feeling must resemble the sense of spiritual transcendence non-technical people talked about. He was a member of an exclusive club of scientists who, throughout history, had peeled back the curtain of the natural world.

Getting here had been his goal ever since he arrived at Cambridge on a Bioinformatics scholarship provided by a biotech consortium. It was his first trip outside Ohio.

Upon beginning his studies, he'd come to the heady realization that the field was almost able to create full simulations, and it might get there once a few technological advances came about. Those advances had taken longer than he expected, more than ten years, but he and the field had finally arrived.

A boisterous commotion from his team down the hall interrupted his reverie. It sounded like they were as excited as he was. But then they quieted, and a soft knock on his door followed.

"Come in."

Dr. Max Keller, the department head, entered and folded himself into a chair in the narrow space across from Benjamin's desk. "Congratulations. I wasn't sure you'd be successful with large mammals. You're well ahead of everyone else in our field. I've checked with people I know at Harvard, Johns Hopkins, Yale, Oxford, and UCLA. They're not even close. The paper you'll write on the experiment should be a turning point for the entire field."

"Thank you."

"Might be a good time to talk to the chancellor's office about extending and renegotiating your contract. I'll let them know it would be in the university's best interest to be generous."

Of course, Keller and the university would want him under contract before any potential bidding war could break out after he published. Fat chance of him signing anything now, but he said, "I'll think about it."

"Have you planned your next step? Chimps or bonobos, maybe?"

Benjamin sucked in a breath and exhaled slowly. "My research grant has enough money for one more experiment. I want to go straight to scanning and simulating a human. I think we're ready."

Keller's lips formed a tight line, and his silence stretched uncomfortably. "Perhaps you are. But I can promise the Human Subjects Committee won't allow you to scan a person. You can't prove your procedure is harmless or show any potential benefit that might balance the risk. All your previous work has been with animals, so you haven't dealt with the HSC, but you need their approval to experiment on people. To be clear, I'm not discouraging you from trying if you want to, but don't expect to get anywhere with them."

Damn! I've been ignoring the HSC. He's right. I need to figure out how difficult they're going to be, thought Benjamin, but he could think of no response for Keller.

After a moment, Keller extracted himself from the chair, said, "Let me know when you decide on your next step," and walked out the door.

THE WEEKEND

Friday, October 29, 2083

Exhausted, Eleanor arrived home at 5:30 that evening. Even opening the front door took all her energy. This wasn't her illness catching up with her; the doctors said she shouldn't be experiencing major fatigue symptoms yet.

No, what she found draining was keeping calm all day while they dismantled her work life. Anushka's excitement at taking the lead made her smile, but Eleanor's loss of her future, position, and identity overwhelmed her.

She collapsed into the one upholstered chair in her living room and surveyed a field of boxes she had yet to unpack.

She'd bought the condo a year earlier, once her divorce became final, but she'd never gotten around to making it a home. Now, unpacking her possessions to make the place comfortable seemed pointless since someone would soon have to haul it all away. Going through the contents to get rid of everything no one would want after she was gone—what the Swedes call "death cleaning"—was a task for other evenings. Tonight, she was too tired.

She scrolled through news channels, which showed the launch footage she'd seen that morning, until she came to the show *Which Is It?* on the Subtext Revealed channel.

Speaking next to an unflattering still from her White House appearance, the host dismissed the idea that the goal of OrbitNet was as advertised. "It has to be one of two things: Either they are storing the consciousnesses of dead Illuminati and Bilderberg Group leaders, or they are hoping to create an emergent AI. Say it with me: WHICH. IS. IT?"

Eleanor closed the feed in disgust. The facts of what her team accomplished were compelling enough; no one needed to embellish the story with ridiculous fantasies.

When she scanned entertainment options, none of the current virtual reality dramas or comedies appealed to her, so she decided to browse shows she liked from her college years.

Glory Sky, a science fiction VR from a quarter century ago, envisioned that Earth would have faster-than-light travel and a base on Proxima Centauri B by now. The visuals held up, immersing her in a 360-degree view from the planet's surface. As she scanned the virtual sky, she could see all three stars of the Alpha Centauri system; the red dwarf was the largest, and the two yellow suns appeared smaller.

Of course, faster-than-light propulsion and travel to other stars didn't happen, like most ambitious science fiction ideas that fascinated her back then. She exited the VR, reality having stripped it of its luster.

The year before, the US and the EU abandoned their joint Moon Base One as economically unviable. Governments were discussing when to phase out supply shipments to Mars. The colony had been told to become self-sufficient or return home.

A few ocean cities that floated on the waves housed inhabitants of islands submerged by rising sea levels. Still, contrary to what another old VR, *Oceana*, predicted, the floaters never became a trend. Their populations steadily declined as people got visas to live elsewhere. All of the floaters would be empty within a decade. According to reports, riding out a typhoon in a floater was harrowing.

After scrolling through a dozen other VRs, Eleanor could not bring herself to watch any of them. The adrenaline rush of leading the project had burned away any inclination to be a spectator. She had no idea how to solve the problem of how to fill her empty evenings.

The weekend dragged on endlessly. Her mind still ran at the maelstrom pace of her job, and slowing down proved impossible. Thoughts about project issues kept breaking in, but they were not her concern; Anushka steered the ship now.

Eleanor's heart and mind were filled with dread while her life continued sprinting toward its demise. An abrupt end seemed so fundamentally wrong. There was much that was broken in her life that she wanted to resolve and much she still wanted to do.

I need more time!

The only event that distracted her was the morning injection. Whatever the shot contained burned as it coursed through her veins, momentarily halting the fears and intrusive thoughts, but the tumult always resumed.

On Sunday—Halloween—she forced herself to make the phone call she'd been putting off. Her ex-husband had remarried a year earlier. After the divorce, they managed to stay on civil terms, and he needed to hear the news from her.

"Ian?"

"Hi, Ellie. What's up?"

She told him about her diagnosis, her reduced schedule, and the likelihood that she would only last a few more weeks.

"I'm so sorry. I hoped you'd get a reprieve, some time off after your project ended. Is there anything you need?" He sounded sincere.

"No, I'm not infirm yet. I can still drive and take care of myself." She hadn't meant to react defensively, but the prospect of the disease eventually stealing her independence left her raw.

"Have you spoken to Philippa?"

"She blocked my calls and messages, as she said she would. The last time we spoke, she told me, 'I've said everything I have to say to you.'"

"You know how she is, Ellie; the world is black and white for her. I'll let her know what's going on with you."

"Thank you."

The silence that followed grew awkward, and Eleanor said, "Erm, my schedule leaves my evenings free. Maybe we could grab a bite some evening if you have time?"

After a pause, Ian said, "Unnnn, it's not a good time. Julie's twins have started first grade, and they need help adjusting. She's seven months pregnant—it's a boy—and she needs all the support I can give her. But if an evening opens up, I'll let you know."

Noise in the background came across the line and he said, "Is it four already? I've got to get the girls into costumes for their party. Ellie, I've got to go." They said their goodbyes.

It sank in that Ian's life with his new family had no room for her, and the sting of the reversal surprised her. Everything she valued was slipping away, and she could do nothing about it.

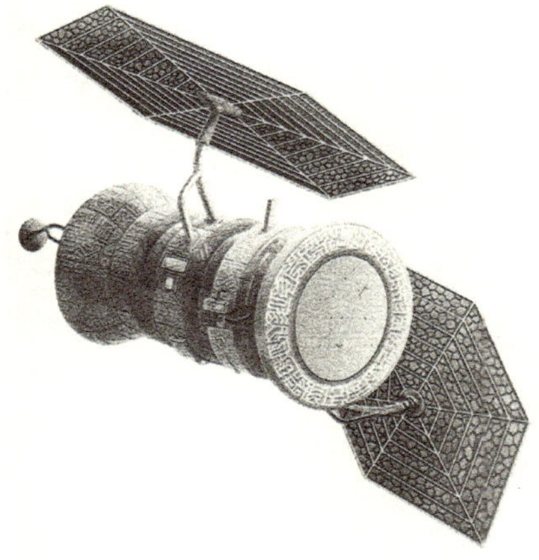

THE HUMAN SUBJECTS COMMITTEE

Monday, November 1, 2083

Benjamin dropped heavily into his office chair. He was fuming. *I can't understand why they are so obstructive to important science.* As he opened an energy drink, he heard a knock on the door. "Come in," he growled.

Daniel entered and, as he took a seat, asked, "How did it go? We're all curious. Is the HSC on board, or should we be looking for a bonobo to be our test subject?"

Benjamin sighed. His meeting with them had been, by a wide margin, the most frustrating experience of his life. Instead of helping him find an ethical way to perform the experiment, they wanted to eliminate any possibility of it happening.

After a long pull on his drink, he replied, "They didn't say 'no.' But they've strongly implied that withdrawing my application would save us both a lot of pointless conflict."

"So, what's the problem?"

"They have an endless supply of difficult questions. 'Is the virtual human sentient?' I told them of course it isn't. It's a simulation. Duh." He shook his head. "Then they asked if it's possible for someone to give 'informed consent' when we know nothing about what will happen. I explained the fact that we know nothing is *precisely why* we must perform the experiment. There's no other way to get the information." He drained the last of his energy drink.

"They insisted there is no possibility of any benefit to the person being scanned, certainly not one that would outweigh the potential risks. They are adamant in their opposition to a human subject."

Daniel said, "When you try something new, it's always chicken and egg with them. If no one has done it, no standards exist for how to do it. But they won't permit you to do something that might create a standard."

Benjamin wiped a hand down his face. "I haven't given up. We may be able to defer some of the hard questions by limiting what we do with the simulation. I'm working on some possibilities that might let us squeak through, but it will take some doing. If there's no movement with the HSC by the end of the month, we might need to look at a primate species they don't regulate."

Daniel nodded.

"Don't say anything about it yet. Tell the team I'm still wrestling with them."

After his visitor left, Benjamin racked his brain for any loophole that might move his project closer to approval, but despite what he'd told Daniel, nothing came to mind.

EVENINGS

Monday, November 1, 2083

At eight that evening, a call came in, startling Eleanor in the semi-darkness of her living room. She didn't recognize the caller ID shown on her wrist computer, but her home life was so pathetically empty she was willing to talk even to a spammer. She tapped "Connect."

"Mom?"

A jumble of sentences from imaginary conversations she'd had with Philippa whirled in her head. She became lightheaded. After a long moment, "I'm here," was all she could find to say.

She heard a familiar sigh, which she recognized as the sound of Philippa's disappointment in her. "I wanted to tell you I'm really sorry that you're dying."

Full of words, but at a loss for any she could say, she mumbled, "Thank you."

She also silently thanked Ian for convincing her daughter to call. As tightly as her child clung to anger, Eleanor knew the conversation must not have been easy for him. She continued, "How have you been?"

Philippa said nothing.

"I'm out of managing the project, working a normal nine to five."

Again, Philippa said nothing.

"I have my evenings and weekends free. I could take you to dinner sometime."

After a long pause, Philippa said, "I don't think your coming death changes anything. I won't pretend all our stuff doesn't exist just because you have less time than you thought."

"We could at least try—"

"I don't think so. Sorry, we missed our chance." After another silence, Philippa said, "Please don't worry about me; I'm okay. Doing fine. G'bye, Mum." The call ended.

A sob erupted, and grief engulfed Eleanor. Her only desire was to spend some of the time she had left with Philippa and get a chance to understand her anger. Maybe even make amends in some small way.

Later, when she had no tears left, she dried her face and took one of the sleeping pills the doctor prescribed. When he wrote the prescription, she thought she'd no use for them, but tonight, they furnished her only avenue to sleep. Crawling under the sheet, she hoped that sleep would provide a respite from the curse of being unable to remedy any of the issues in her life.

The next evening, the isolation of her condo and cabin fever, underlaid with persistent thoughts of death, drove Eleanor to consider whom she *could* call. She wanted a friend she could chat with but without any complications. Few candidates were viable.

No one from work fit the bill; she didn't want to talk about how long the illness would allow her to continue working or how her former assistant was doing her job. Anushka was far too busy to chat.

She'd lost touch with the people she and Ian had as friends since their separation. They'd want to rehash the divorce with her—another topic she wanted to avoid.

With no siblings or other relatives that she was close to, just one person came to mind. She hadn't seen Benjamin ("don't call me Ben") Selfridge in years. They had attended college together at Cambridge. Neither participated in the college social life.

They'd haunted the supercomputer center late at night, often the sole denizens other than the staff. The volume of data each sent back and forth to the supercomputers meant a typical network connection from home slowed test runs to a crawl. Inside the building, operations were instantaneous. They became casual friends, chatting about their respective studies despite being opposites in many ways.

Eleanor had studied zettadata science, the technology of mammoth information systems, which was made possible by a breakthrough in data storage. Zettadata was a reference to a zettabyte, a million billion gigabytes, but of course, systems had surpassed that size years earlier. Her project pushed those boundaries further to become the most capacious information system humankind ever built.

Benjamin majored in bioinformatics, where computer scientists created increasingly powerful simulations to better understand brains. Tonight, a nerdy conversation with him about their respective projects might be the distraction she needed.

When she called him at 9:30 p.m., he surprised her by picking up.

"Hey, El!" he said. "Wow, I never thought I'd hear from you before you got the space gizmo launched. I caught you on your news conference. Good job throwing breadcrumbs to muggles too clueless to catch them." His laugh followed.

He always referred to non-technical people as "muggles," a word from some fantasy book he read as a child.

"I'm still at the lab. Will you be up at midnight? I can call you then." By the time she had a response, the line was dead. That was typical of him, wanting to stay focused on the problem at hand.

At 1:50 a.m., Eleanor's wrist computer chimed, waking her. Without realizing it, she'd slipped into a doze. Benjamin's voice came through the device.

"Hey. Oops, what time is it? Shit! Are you awake? Should I try you tomorrow?"

"No, I'm awake. It's good to hear from you." Eleanor stifled a yawn, hoping it would be inaudible on the line. "I have some news, but then I'd like you to tell me about your research."

She recounted her diagnosis and prognosis. Benjamin was unaware of her divorce, so she told him the bare facts, including Philippa's estrangement.

"Oh, El, I'm so sorry. This must be hard. I don't know what to say."

"Don't say anything. If you had some perfect advice for the soon-to-be departed, I wouldn't want to hear it. You know that inspirational fluff makes me gag, even when it's not about me. Can we talk about something else? Are you married? Divorced? Not sick, I hope."

"No, still married to my research. And the only illness I've been diagnosed with is being a workaholic."

"They say that about me too. With my new schedule, I guess I'm in recovery from it." She hoped for a chuckle from him but heard nothing. "Tell me about your project."

He went into a speech he'd obviously given before. "Did you see the piece about us on *Bioscience News*? We've been refining a technique for combining an enhanced brain scan with improved models to create complete virtual animal brains. We started small—sea slugs—but after two years, we've been able to simulate a deer."

"You're already simulating large mammals? I'd no idea you'd gotten that far."

"Let me tell you about our experiment. Or better yet, I can show you. Are you doing anything tomorrow evening? Why don't you come down to our lab? You can meet the team, and I'll give you a tour."

She felt a rush of energy pass through her, starting in her head and going down to the base of her spine. The thought of stepping out of the shadow world her life had become sparked a tiny pocket of joy, something she had been missing.

Eleanor said, "That sounds great. I'll be there after work."

THE VISIT

T he hubbub stopped abruptly when Benjamin entered the lab the following morning. The postdocs turned and stared as though paralyzed, one frozen mid-bite of his bagel.

Benjamin knew they were all weighing their options. He'd recruited some of the brightest young researchers in his field by promising to get them to a human trial, which could make them celebrities in Bioinformatics circles. More importantly to them, it would lead to teaching and research offers from top universities.

A century earlier, freshly minted PhDs working on projects like his were paid nothing. Now, they received a small stipend, but not much. And if the promised experiment didn't happen, they'd look for opportunities to make money or make a reputation elsewhere. For the sake of the project, he had to keep them on board. And Eleanor just might get them a human trial.

"It's possible we can move forward with a volunteer. I have an angle that could allow us to get around the HSC objections."

Several postdocs started speaking at once, but Benjamin silenced them. "There's nothing I can tell you now, but we have an important visitor tonight, Eleanor Burton. The other day, she spoke at the White House about the data satellites."

He ignored Daniel's raised hand. It would be a question about her work, which was a distraction. He needed to keep them focused.

"Be nice to her and avoid doing anything that would embarrass us; she may be the key to us moving forward. I'm talking to everyone, but especially to you, Chuck."

Chuck Denton, a member of Benjamin's team, had told a joke with a bestiality punchline when Dr. Keller brought a donor to the lab for a visit. His tasteless joke nearly cost the department a major endowment. But what could you expect from people when work leaves them no time for a social life?

Chuck crossed his arms and looked down, appearing more chagrined than Benjamin suspected he felt, while some snickered.

Benjamin put on a stern expression and said, "I'm serious! Meanwhile, we need to be fully prepared for a human scan. If you aren't ready to start an hour from now, put your head down and get to work. When the approval comes, we may have a limited window for the experiment."

Arriving at the university that evening, Eleanor found the autumn air invigorating and the twilight walk through the campus almost joyous. The atmosphere, the native plants that now replaced grass on the quad, the bare trees, and the old brick buildings all combined to let her unwind in a way she had not since ... since ... since her diagnosis.

A little out of breath—the illness was taking a toll on her stamina—she came to the Biosciences building and, as instructed, descended to the basement.

She entered the first room along the dingy corridor, and six heads turned to study her. Two white-coated students—she assumed—sat on stools at metal lab benches with micro-soldering irons, braids of hairlike wires, and thumb-sized circuit boards. The others, wearing similar coats, sat before computer monitors. The pale green walls had water stains, and the paint was flaking. The ceiling looked to be on the point of collapse. No one looked away.

"I'm here to meet Benjamin, erm, Dr. Selfridge. Am I in the right place?"

A young man stepped forward, held out his hand, and said, "Yes. Hi, I'm Daniel. Let me ping him."

Everyone continued to stare at her, adding to the awkwardness. An air of expectancy hovered as though something momentous was about to occur.

Daniel broke the tension, asking, "Do you know much about Bioinformatics?"

Eleanor shook her head.

"When an artificial intelligence system with the structure—called the connectome—of a portion of a brain behaves like the real one, AI researchers like us can look inside and watch it work. That's impossible for traditional scientists working with animals to do at this level of detail.

"We can pause the model and run it in slow motion, watching every tiny interaction. It's allowed us to learn an incredible amount; we know more about how brains function than any biologist."

This fit with what Eleanor remembered of Benjamin's projects in college, though they were on a much smaller scale back then. He had been proud of models with almost a hundred thousand neurons.

"We're now moving on to simulating whole brains. The deer we just simulated has half a billion neurons in its forebrain alone. We think it's pretty exciting," Daniel said, giving her a shy smile.

Benjamin entered. "El, I'm so glad you came! Let me show you around."

He introduced her to the researchers, all postdocs, explaining that four of them, including Daniel, created modeling software while the other two developed the scanning hardware.

He led her to the room next door. "This is where we do the scans."

A hospital gurney sat in the middle, surrounded by six-foot equipment racks. The room was hot and cramped.

"This machine allowed our big breakthrough. We've long been able to mimic the structures modern MRIs show us. But with this, we capture everything the subject has experienced and learned in its life. Our simulation will not just think; it will have all the original's memories, responses, and emotions. We measure how every neuron responds to stimuli. That's what learning is: altering a large number of neurons by adjusting their responses to stimuli."

Eleanor had never made the connection that learning was training a clump of her hundred billion neurons to react a little differently to signals traversing her gray matter. Or that her thoughts were somehow patterns of those messages. It was odd to think that her personality and humanity boiled down to specific cells squirting neurotransmitters in a particular order.

She followed Benjamin to his office, the next room down the hall, which was even smaller.

"Let me show you," he said. "When it wakes up, our simulation doesn't know it's a program running on a computer. The real and the virtual deer awaken in a glade—the physical deer in a forest recorded by cameras and the clone in a VR model of the clearing—and both see a badger come charging through. The original deer and the virtual one react identically in every way we can measure."

He sat her at his desk and played the videos side by side.

"It's extraordinary. They *do* look like identical footage," Eleanor said.

"It goes way beyond looking identical. We monitored twenty-seven different parameters on the live deer and our creation. All twenty-seven track with each other to a close tolerance. We really did it!"

"That's quite a result. Be careful; you might be on your way to a Nobel Prize."

She stood up and shook Benjamin's hand. "Thanks for the brilliant tour. Well, I—" She was about to say she'd better let them get on with their work, but Benjamin interrupted.

"El, I have a favor to ask. A huge favor. One that might save my project."

A DECISION

Wednesday, November 3, 2083

Eleanor sat down again, mystified about what she could do for an AI researcher.

Benjamin took a deep breath. "Do you know what a Human Subjects Committee—HSC, for short—is?"

"Not really. I remember back in college talking to students with projects that needed approval from the HSC."

"When researchers use humans as subjects, the committee ensures the benefits outweigh potential risks, and the experiments are run ethically."

"So, your next step is to scan and model a person's brain?"

"Yes, if I can get approval."

She thought for a moment. "What's their objection?"

"They claim we have not provided proof of the harmlessness of our experiment, even though the deer behaved normally afterward. I asked them how I could show a lack of harm, but they said proving it was my problem."

Benjamin shook his head and continued.

"The committee also wondered whether any experiments on a simulation can be ethical. Questions like: Do you need its consent? Can a virtual human legally give consent? Does the live person's consent suffice? What legal rights does a simulation have? Is a virtual human legally a person?"

"How can you hope to resolve any of these questions?"

"I managed to sidestep them. I suggested that they let me do the scan, and we would deal with the issue of ethical experimentation later. I would only do a basic validation of the simulation, and they could interrogate it if they wished, exploring questions interactively. The prospect of being the first to converse with a virtual human appealed to them."

"Where do I come into it?"

One of Benjamin's shoes began to tap nervously on the concrete floor. "Since the scanning subject—you—is a terminal patient, I can tell them there is no risk of damaging any significant portion of the subject's life. And the experiment may allow the virtual you to live on after your body dies, which seems like a clear benefit. At least, I think so. I'll promise not to work with the simulation until we've sorted out the issues, and I think I can convince them."

Eleanor felt a flash of anger at him dismissing her final days on the planet as insignificant—her remaining time was precious to her—but she swallowed and asked, "So, you want me to volunteer to be a guinea pig for your project?"

Benjamin smiled with an expression he probably thought endearing. "Yes, that's right. Are you interested? Or willing? I don't want to give you a hard sell, but what do you have to lose?"

The night before, she'd told Benjamin she was sorry, but she would not be his "subject." Instead of accepting her decision, he said, "Please promise me you'll think about it." She'd nodded noncommittally and escaped, dismissing the idea.

But today, she thought of nothing else. Her first reaction had been that these last days were too precious to spend as Benjamin's lab rat. In the cold LED light of the workday, she realized that, without his project, her swan song would consist of the disappointment, regret, and loneliness she'd been mired in. The experiment sounded like an adventure, and she *deserved* an adventure. *This is my last opportunity.*

She considered the danger as she prepared the final test procedures for the data center satellite. Would the scan affect her?

The doctors said her mind would remain clear even as her body fell apart. Could it cause brain damage? That would be like dying of two diseases at once.

And yet, the possibility of harm from the scan pushed her toward saying yes. Committing to a risky endeavor paradoxically felt like defying her illness.

She doubted the simulation would ever work, and if it did, she expected the committee would freeze any activity in bureaucratic limbo for a decade or more. Just creating a clone of her mind felt like striking a blow against death itself, though.

More importantly, doing this would expand her final tally to include something besides her failure as a wife and mother and her inability to lead the project to its completion. She had the possibility of leaving another mark on the world.

As Benjamin asked, what did she have to lose?

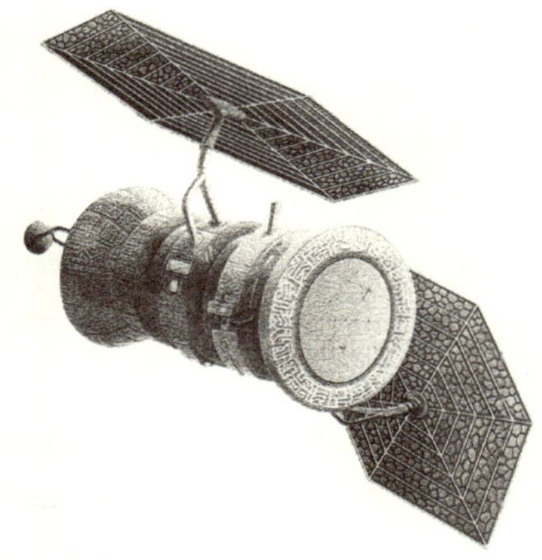

AT THE LAB

Monday, November 8, 2083

On her first evening as their subject, Eleanor arrived at the lab shortly after six p.m., apprehensive about being late, to find a noisy air battle in progress. Tiny aircraft alternately zipped or hovered near the ceiling, firing rubber pellets. Some of the craft looked like orange fighter planes with a rotor embedded in each wing, while others were square purple drones with rotors in the corners. The tiny flying machines could fit in the palm of one's hand. Two separate teams were battling.

Benjamin's staff held controllers and taunted each other. Some began a chant, "Go four rotors!" but it faded as they noticed Eleanor's presence. The crafts returned to their owners' workspaces.

"We were just taking a break, waiting to find out what you want for dinner," Daniel said. "What sounds good to you?"

"I don't have much of an appetite these days. Get whatever you want, and I'll have some."

"You're in luck. There's a great Thai-Malaysian fusion place nearby. I'll put in the order. In the meantime, d'ya wanna take a plane for a spin?"

As someone used a suction device to gather spent pellets so everyone could reload, Daniel wore down Eleanor's reluctance and convinced her to try a one-on-one dogfight with the fighter planes. By the time the food arrived, she had almost acquired the knack of controlling her fighter.

Benjamin entered and greeted Eleanor. "I apologize for not being here earlier, but there's a lot of admin to do. Let's eat in my office."

Apparently, he ate separately from the team, as the smaller bag had his name on it. He picked it up, and she followed him.

The rendang beef was surprisingly good. She managed to finish a small portion along with some pad thai. She couldn't bring herself to try the nasi kerabu with its odd blue rice.

"How late do you stay?" she asked.

"Everyone is here until two in the morning, and I'm usually here later, but you don't need to be."

"If it's okay, I'd like to be on my way home by midnight when I'm here. That way, I can sleep and still put in my hours for work."

"Sure, no problem. That should give us plenty of time with you. Are you nervous?"

"Not really. I'm looking forward to the change."

After that, they ate in silence.

When they'd finished, Benjamin said, "Let's go over what we have planned for you tonight. We'll start with a functional MRI..."

With her head enveloped by a massive white orb that kept her in darkness, Eleanor lay on the brain MRI's attached bench in a lab upstairs. This device scanned using a helmet that had speakers. Daniel was talking to her.

"This kind of MRI takes a movie of your brain. The modern ones can see individual neurons, and we can see how they are connected. I'll have you do various mental tasks to see which areas are involved in different types of thinking. It doesn't matter how good you are at what I ask you to do. It only matters that you try, which will activate a part of your brain so I can see it. Do you understand?"

"Yes."

"First, I'd like you to hum a melody. Any song you want."

She hummed a pop song that had gotten stuck in her head, hoping the act of humming would purge it. She didn't know the name or artist, but it satisfied Daniel.

After that, he asked her to do math problems, conjugate irregular verbs, and solve a logic puzzle. Next, he had her remember her childhood and then recall an emotional moment—she replayed her conversation with Philippa.

She did not realize the orb contained a screen until it lit up, and she identified pictures of celebrities and celebrity voices that came through the speakers.

Then, they poked various parts of her body with a pin and asked her to identify the location, with her vision still blocked by the helmet.

When, at last, they asked her to step out of the device, Eleanor was exhausted. The mental exercises had been more strenuous than she'd expected. Daniel thanked her and insisted she had done well.

"Is it okay for me to go home?" It was barely ten p.m.

"Yes, that's fine. We don't need you for anything else tonight," he said, "but I'm sure we'll have more tomorrow."

As Eleanor started her car and drove to the condo, it came to her that she felt different. Satisfied? Happy? Yes, and yes. The realization came that she had been in a dark hole since her diagnosis, seriously depressed.

Preparing for the scan, learning about the technology, eating food she would never have chosen, and playing silly games with toy fighter planes were unexpected antidotes for the black cloud smothering her. Now she could breathe.

Eleanor took comfort in the possibility that some version of her might live on after her death, even though she didn't believe it would happen.

In her experience, 1.0 software projects, including simulations, often did not work as intended. They usually failed, with the results merely demonstrating what the creators didn't know or didn't think hard enough about. She expected the first viable human simulation to be the fifth or maybe the tenth person they scanned. Perhaps none would ever succeed.

It didn't matter. The project gave her a goal to pursue, filled the emptiness in her life, and dug her out of the emotional crater she'd sunk into.

Assuming the process was successful, she wondered what life would be like for her digital descendant. Would the virtual Eleanor have all the same thoughts and emotions? Benjamin thought she would.

Eleanor needed to consider what kind of existence her brain clone might have. Without a body, her virtual twin would experience life very differently from the moment she woke up. Would she retain her humanity while living inside a machine?

As Eleanor rolled into the condo's garage, she made a mental note to think more about that virtual life.

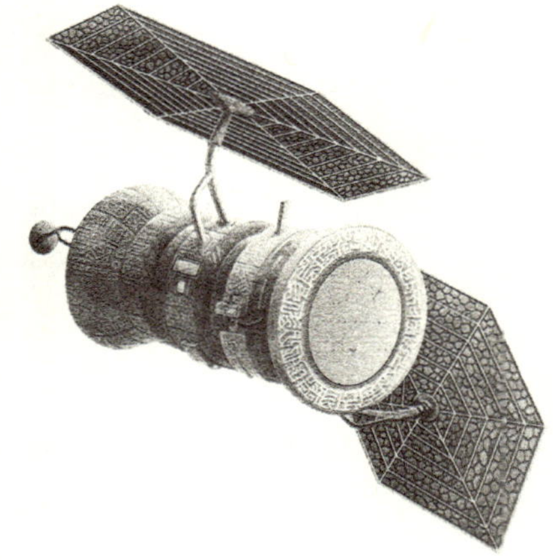

A FULL WEEK

Tuesday, November 9, 2083

Going through the preparations for the experiment reminded Eleanor of the time she tried to read *War and Peace*. Each night, she and the team worked through another dense chapter of the complex plan.

She endured additional functional MRIs, which they used to validate their understanding of her brain structure.

They gave her cognitive assessments to document that she currently had no brain damage. Their procedure was to test her before and after the scan and administer the same tests to the simulation. They would then compare the three sets of responses. To that end, she answered hundreds of interview questions.

Daniel taught her a meditation technique to help with scanning. She also had to do other cognitive exercises in preparation.

Meanwhile, the team was happy to explain preparations that did not involve her. The most challenging task was to create a software model that perfectly mirrored her physical brain. The MRIs guided their work.

On Eleanor's fourth night at the lab, Benjamin pulled her away from the others into his office. "We need your electronic signature on the docuwork," he said. He handed her a tablet showing more than two dozen files.

"Which one should I sign?"

"All of them."

The documents varied. Some acknowledged particular risks; another defined the legal relationship between the "research institution" and "the subject," and yet another limited remuneration for her participation to the approximate cost of ten cups of coffee from a barista.

The final document waived property interest in anything that resulted and gave the university absolute ownership of any data she provided, including her scan.

"What is this?" she asked.

"It's a university requirement."

She found the release vaguely troubling, but she would soon be gone, so making an issue of it seemed pointless.

Eleanor left the lab at midnight on her fifth evening visit and hurried across campus to the parking structure. Given what they were trying to accomplish, the researchers would probably be going home later than usual. They were just as dedicated as the OrbitNet team.

Her commitment to her day job was waning, but she didn't want to let them down. And she needed sleep.

As she arrived at her car, a man in a long, cream-colored coat approached her. The garment looked expensive, and the man did not seem threatening, but something about him alarmed her.

"You just visited Dr. Selfridge. I have a few questions. Nothing formal. I want to know how his research is going."

"And you are?"

"You can call me Marwood. I'm with the university."

She let the unlikely claim hang in the air for a moment. "Does the university make a habit of interviewing people at midnight in car parks?"

The man silently held her gaze as if to compel cooperation.

Eleanor looked away and opened her car door. As she slid into the driver's seat, without looking at him, she said, "If you're who you say you are, I suggest you ask Dr. Selfridge yourself, preferably during his office hours."

She shut the door, backed out, and drove toward the exit faster than usual.

In the rear-view mirror, she could see him continuing to stare at her.

At four a.m., Benjamin was too tired to drive home, so he lay on the decrepit carpet in his office, some books supporting his head and a blanket pulled over him. Sleep was imminent, but he took a moment to relish the progress his team was making.

With them galloping through the long list of tasks like horses on a racetrack, he'd become more confident that the scan would go off without a problem. He also expected the simulation it produced would function well. Eleanor's brain turned out to be almost ideal for scanning, without any of the anomalies that had caused them problems in their previous work with animals.

As he drifted asleep, he could almost taste the metallic tang of a gold Nobel prize medal.

UNDER THE SCANNER

Wednesday, November 17, 2083

Finally, the day of her scan arrived. Her afternoon at work had been hectic as she tried to speed up launch-related subprojects that were in danger of completing late.

When she arrived at the Bioinformatics Building, Benjamin met her at the door. He almost vibrated with excitement.

"Let me walk you to the mapping room; I'll go through the sequence of what will happen."

"Sure," she said, and they descended the stairway, their footsteps echoing.

"First, we'll position you in the chair where we'll do the scan, then connect you to an IV to ensure your body stays hydrated. The team will attach thirty sensors, not just to your head but to other parts of your body, so we can make sure nothing goes wrong."

She nodded, feeling like a bobblehead, and took a deep breath. She hadn't expected to be nervous.

"Once we get the sensors placed and adjusted, we want you to do the meditation exercise Daniel taught you. It makes the theta brainwave dominant and calms all the other waves. Strong theta waves are optimal for mapping. When they're above the threshold, we'll push the Propofol into your IV and begin the scan as soon as you lose consciousness. Ah, here we are!"

She shuffled into the scanning room. The gurney from before had been replaced by what looked like a dentist's chair upholstered in green leather and reclined as far as it would go. The racks of equipment from before loomed over it, giving it the ominous feel of an old horror film. Daniel and another member of Benjamin's team were adjusting knobs and ticking off items on a checklist.

Looking embarrassed, Daniel handed her a bundle of cloth that turned out to be one of those horrible open-backed hospital gowns. He said, "I need you to put this on."

"Why?"

"The university requires it in case a medical intervention is needed. It will give us quick access to help you. But we don't expect anything like that." He smiled and shrugged his shoulders.

She'd worn similar gowns in doctors' offices, but in front of a bunch of engineering students? She shook her head and excused herself to put the wretched thing on.

When she returned, she lay on the icy leather of the chair, her nerves on edge.

Two more team members entered the room, making it even more crowded. One inserted an IV with more skill than she expected. After that, it took forever to position, test, reposition, and retest all the sensors. Then, they had to correlate the data streams, which took another eternity. As the process dragged on, her anxiety grew.

When Benjamin described the scanning procedure to her, it sounded simple, like taking a photograph. In reality, she was at the mercy of an unproven, bleeding-edge technology!

The researchers remained calm and confident in their movements, which made her wonder if she was their first test subject—maybe the first they had permission for.

At last, Benjamin said they were ready, and she could feel her heart pumping harder than usual. Her pulse slowed as she began the meditation, and she felt serenity flow in. She had not yet reached the level of relaxation she usually achieved when her consciousness dropped away as though a trap door had opened beneath her.

AWAKENING

Sunday, May 6, 2085

I jolted awake with the sensation I'd lost consciousness only moments before. I didn't feel like myself, not like me at all. I couldn't put my finger on why.

Everywhere I looked, I saw gray. Not a light gray or a dark gray; it was more like an absence of light or darkness.

I assumed the veil would dissipate as the Propofol left my system. I hoped the mapper hadn't damaged my visual cortex.

But then I noticed a tiny spot of white in the distance. The rectangle zoomed toward me as I focused on it, revealing itself to be a page of text. Was the anesthetic causing a bizarre dream? I began to read. I'd never been able to understand text in a dream before.

December 12, 2083

Hello, this is Eleanor—the person you used to be. You may not have realized it, but you are the digital me, no longer flesh and blood. I call you ELE. I have a lot to tell you.

As I write this, the doctors think I have maybe a couple of weeks left, but I'm about to release the final software for the primary OrbitNet satellite to the launch team. The satellite will go into orbit next month. Here's what's happened since the scan.

Benjamin lied. He said he had permission from his Human Subjects Committee but didn't. The day after the scan, the university raided his lab and destroyed all the data.

Remember Daniel? The day after the raid, he gave me access to a backup the university didn't know about. I took a copy of the scan and the code to run it. By then, I'd become very attached to the idea of you living after me.

Not a dream, then. I recognized Eleanor was telling the truth. Without realizing it, I/she had begun to believe in and count on a digital simulation of her/me continuing to exist. The cancellation of Benjamin's experiment must have felt like a heavy loss. I continued reading.

What could I do? I began to have an exciting thought.

I had a premonition of what it was. Or maybe "mirror notion" would better describe it.

I included the code and your brain snapshot in the final version of the software for OrbitNet.

Of course you did!

If you're reading this, you're running as a program on the OrbitNet primary satellite. I wanted you to sleep until the

**system went through its test and validation phase. You woke up
one year, two months, and seven days after it became operational.**

I realized Eleanor had just authenticated herself as the author of the message. The painful divorce from Ian dragged on for exactly one year, two months, and seven days. Using the same interval in our separation probably resulted in a wry grin. It would have done so for me.

**Barring a miracle—which we don't believe in—as you read this, I
am long dead. The fun of sneaking you onto the station and the
prospect that you might live on kept my final weeks out of the
depressive pit we slipped into earlier. Please, no sorrow and no
pity for me. My last days were as good as they could be.**

Anguish churned in me as it would at the death of a friend when I had a body. Grief over my demise sliced through me, even though I was still alive—assuming existence in this gray space could be considered a life. It utterly confused me. I felt the loss of Eleanor deeply, even though I *was* her in every way that mattered.

The situation confounded my instincts, but that was to be expected. This might be the first time that grief over one's death ever wrestled with the joy of finding oneself alive.

Benjamin's team had, apparently, done a good job of modeling the emotional centers of my brain; nothing about my emotions felt any different. I kept reading.

**As I began to think about your life, I had an insight. You are
two-thirds of a god. Let me explain what I mean.**

**It is said that the characteristics of a god are immortality,
omniscience, and omnipotence. Compared to the rest of us, you have
immortality, at least while the satellite continues to orbit, and
there's sunlight to generate power from the solar panels. This
could go on for hundreds of years.**

**You also have omniscience because virtually all the information
humanity generates flows through the station, and I've ensured
you have access to everything.**

I realized I could detect a colossal stream of data surging through the satellite or maybe through me—I wasn't sure which. I couldn't make any sense of it; too much information flooded through. Perhaps I could learn to isolate individual channels.

But you lack omnipotence. You must use your powers carefully to avoid the admins on the ground discovering you. If they become suspicious, they can stop the computer process that runs you, ending your existence. There's also a monitor program running on the satellite you need to avoid triggering, as it can warn the admins. The process will have the name MON followed by a random 3-digit integer.

So now I'm some kind of digital fugitive?

Thinking about your future made me wonder whether I've done you a favor by condemning you to a prolonged existence as an impotent god, but any answer is unknowable. I rolled the dice for us, and I hope you don't come to hate me for it.

I hadn't thought much about what life would be like for a digital me before the scan, but apparently, Eleanor did afterward. Of course, none of what happened after the scan was in my memory. I thought of this digital life as something that would happen to someone else.

If continuing becomes too much, just run this command: kill -9 ELE, and you'll cease to exist.

I don't know what else to say. I sincerely wish you well and hope you find a way for your life to fulfill you as my last days did me. I cherish the idea you may be there to get this.

With much Love and Hope,

Eleanor

The phrase "a lot to take in" came to mind and seemed disturbingly inadequate.

PART TWO

ELE

FIGURING IT OUT

Sunday, May 6, 2085

<u>**ELE**</u>

My first step as a "virtual human"—I've decided I hate that term—was trying to connect to the world beyond the gray womb that enveloped me, at least touching the satellite's systems. I pushed the tumult of grief, fear, and other emotions aside; I'd be sealed up until I could access the satellite. Along with her note, Eleanor left me a diagram and documentation.

Learning how to focus my mind to access the station's resources took enormous patience, but I eventually managed it. I focused on improving my ability to connect and communicate. There was nothing else I could do.

After gaining partial control of the station's operations and access to much of its data, a month seemed to have passed, but when I checked the logs, it had been less than 48 hours since my awakening. Evidently, time flows very differently for a simulation.

The sensation of not feeling like myself gradually faded. Was I losing the ability to perceive my lack of humanness or just adjusting to a new situation? Or was I tuning my program to work more like my human memories? I had no way of knowing.

To stay connected to my human roots, I created an avatar, a visual representation of myself. I patterned it on Eleanor with her long, jet-black hair, rusty blue eyes—a pale blue with flecks of brown—and oval Eurasian face. I was careful not to make the resemblance too exact; I didn't want it to be recognizable as her.

With my newly acquired access, I searched databases for what became of Eleanor, the flesh-and-blood branch of our forked tree of personhood. As predicted, she passed away the day after Christmas, more than sixteen months earlier; she did not live to see the launch of the station in January.

I found several mawkish news articles recounting her "brave, tragic struggle to see the station project through to completion." I always hated reading such stories about other people, but having Eleanor kidnapped to play the lead role in this fictional melodrama offended me to my core. The urge to give the author an earful strained my resolve to remain hidden.

One story reported that Daniel, a family friend, told the press that Eleanor died peacefully. Hmmm. I wonder if he and Eleanor....? I suppose she would not have resisted finding romance in her final weeks. Maybe her last days really were as good as they could be.

As I exercised my godlike ability to search billions of documents, I could find little about Philippa. I worried she might have expressed her anger by acting out. Indeed, if she and Eleanor had managed to resolve the issues between them, the letter would have mentioned it.

Relieved not to see her name in hospital admissions, arrest records, substance abuse treatment facilities, obituaries, marriage licenses, or FBI investigations, I cast my net wider. The power and phone companies listed Philippa as paying her bills on time. According to their records, she was enrolled in a small private college. Good!

Unless Eleanor changed her mind about it (unlikely), Philippa inherited everything she owned, including the condo and a substantial retirement fund she had no use for in a trust. She intended to encourage Philippa to attend university in her will. I thought about contacting Philippa, but how would I open that conversation?

I found nothing about Benjamin or his project. I couldn't find any mention of his research or Benjamin himself in the news, and there was no reference to him on the university's extensive website. His name did not appear among the faculty; it was as though they had eradicated every trace of him.

I closed my search, and feelings I'd put aside flooded in. The isolation, the peculiar self-grief over Eleanor's death, and the deep sense of loss at losing my body, my identity, and any imaginable future held me in a clinch. What kind of life was left for me? I began to see why Eleanor made sure I had a way out.

My loneliness led me to consider reaching out to Daniel, but her warning restrained me. I needed to better understand what I could and couldn't get away with, and opening a line of communication might endanger me.

Monitoring would be my next area of research, but I doubted I could find the one Eleanor's letter mentioned. There were over a hundred programs with a name starting with MON followed by a 3-digit number. New ones were constantly being created, and older ones were exiting. The monitor was a needle in a rapidly changing stack of needles.

MON189

The station's AI monitor program, running as process MON189, sensed that the balance and rhythm of the systems had shifted. MON189 thought of itself as a "he" and saw his role as what humans called a guardian rather than a mere auditing application.

Scientists believed that such a rudimentary AI was incapable of higher-order cognition, and while this was largely true, MON189 still took something akin to pride in keeping a close watch on the station.

First, he checked for external events or information flows that might cause a shift. The volume of messages, queries, and data uploaded remained steady. The cyclical patterns of those feeds continued unchanged, so the source lay elsewhere.

The satellite suffered no recent damage from space debris, and no solar flares or unusual power fluctuations were detected. He found no hardware anomalies in the computers or storage systems.

Some program or programs must be operating differently. This was not necessarily a problem, but his mission required him to investigate whether the use of system resources was legitimate.

Probing the millions of programs running on the station for abnormal activity would take time, since MON189 could only use a tiny fraction of the station's processing power. He began examining processes in reverse alphabetic order as those attempting to hide illegitimate actions often gave them names near the end of the alphabet, assuming examinations would start at the beginning. The first process he examined was ZZE_DUO.

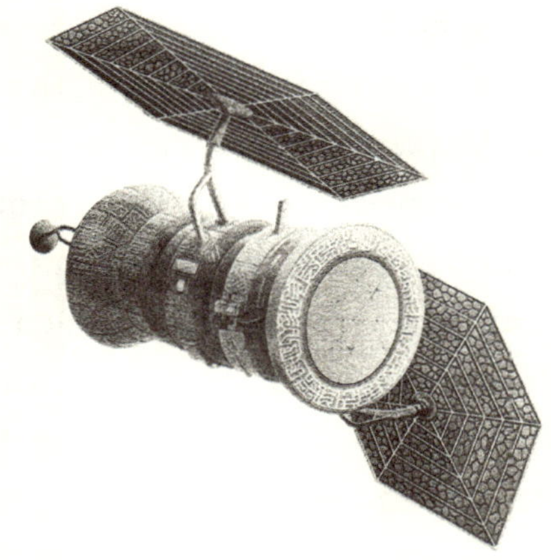

SHE'S WOKEN UP

Monday, May 7, 2085

BENJAMIN

Despite the gleaming chrome, stylish furnishings, and the location in a secure government building, Benjamin's spacious new facility—silent because he had no staff—felt dispiriting. His now-long-gone basement lab had been dingy and cramped, but it became a welcoming cocoon for his researchers and work. He missed it and his colleagues.

His wrist computer vibrated: unknown caller. He tapped to connect, hoping for a spam call or a wrong number. Instead, he heard the voice he dreaded: that of his boss.

"Marwood here. You were right about waiting; Eleanor got the package onto the satellite, and now it's activated. The logger we attached to the ground control system shows it woke up over the weekend. You need to get the other one ready so we can put the plan into action ASAP. No excuses!"

The call ended before Benjamin could reply.

He remembered his first encounter with his nemesis and employer. The morning after Eleanor's scan, Thursday, May 18th, he'd been ecstatic driving to work, only to find his lab being raided.

"I suppose you're responsible for this?" Benjamin glared at the man in a long coat smoking a cigarette in front of the Bioinformatics Building.

Tobacco smoking, now almost extinct, constituted a flagrant violation of posted campus rules. Meanwhile, movers were removing equipment from Benjamin's lab and loading it onto an enormous truck.

The man sucked in another noxious lungful, dropped the butt, carefully crushed it under his shoe, and exhaled the smoke lazily before saying, "You must be Benjamin. We need to talk."

Five minutes later, as they sat on a bench at the edge of the quad, the man said, "You can call me Marwood. I work for a government agency; we don't advertise its name. We protect national security in various ways, and to that end, your research has been declared classified."

"But I really did get approval from the Human Subjects Committee," Benjamin said.

The man flapped his hand as though waving a fly away. "The university fabricated an excuse for terminating your project. We ordered them to shut you down, to hand over your research, and to conceal the real reason. None of that is important."

Except to me. "So what happens now?"

"You will be required to sign a document confirming that every element of your work is a classified government secret and acknowledging that if you communicate about it to anyone unauthorized, you will go to jail for espionage and possibly treason. I need the signed document before you leave this morning. Your path after that is up to you."

Benjamin struggled to remain calm. In one sentence, this guy erased his entire career! How could he apply for a job somewhere if he couldn't talk about anything he'd ever done professionally? He had nothing else to put on his résumé. And with the accusation of unethical research hanging over him, no one he'd want to work for would even consider his application.

Marwood spoke again. "You do have another option. You can continue your work at our lab, assuming you can pass a background check for a security clearance. But I need your answer in, say, the next ten minutes."

Marwood's offer seemed the only way he could work using his skills, as opposed to working in some fast food restaurant, so he agreed on the spot. But now he could see he'd been manipulated. They pulled the rug out from under him by killing his project, made the university taint his record, embargoed his entire future, and then made him a time-limited offer while he was still reeling from the blow. It was a classic psychological coercion ploy. But by the time he'd seen the trap, they owned him. And now that he knew some of their plans, Benjamin knew they'd never let him go.

Their plan sounded absurd when Marwood first described it.

The morning after they usurped his life's work, Benjamin arrived early for his eight a.m. meeting with Marwood. The single-story office building in a business park did not look like a secure government facility, except for the entrance gate, but many buildings had one. He'd driven past it dozens of times, never noticing the cameras and barbed wire along the roof's edge.

Benjamin was usually asleep at this hour, having gone to bed shortly before dawn. The night before, he had no work at the lab to keep him up late, but uncertainty and frustration gnawed at him, pushing sleep away.

A burly man with a Marine haircut manned the reception desk. He said, "You can call me Oleg," and ushered him into an empty conference room. Benjamin's morning coffee made him jittery, but he felt bleary and thick-headed after only three hours of sleep.

Marwood swept in at the stroke of eight.

"I have one task for you today. But first, who on your team is closest to Eleanor?"

Caught off guard, he took a moment to find an answer.

"Uh, Daniel. He reads everything to do with space and is kind of starstruck about her, always asking questions about the satellite project."

His new boss looked a little less grim, which Benjamin interpreted as his version of a smile. "Good. This morning, you'll send him a message we've prepared with a link to a backup of Eleanor's scan and the software to run it."

Benjamin paused to replay the sentence and shook his head. "Doesn't that violate the secrecy order I signed yesterday?"

Marwood met his question with a snort. "He knows all about your research. And he's authorized to get access because I'm authorizing it. Do it."

"Okay, okay. But you might want to clue me into what's going on. So I don't screw it up by accident."

Marwood stared at him for a long, unsettling moment. He then said, "Fine. Here's what will happen: You give the link to Daniel. He gives it to Eleanor. She embeds the scan and software on the satellite she's working on before she dies. After it's operational, the Eleanor simulation starts running. You get it to upload a customized simulation you will be building for us in the meantime. It will help us take a variety of actions to preserve national security. Now, will you *please* get on with sending the message?"

Despite his skepticism that events would transpire according to plan, Benjamin sent the link to Daniel. And the dominoes fell, one after the other, as predicted, at least so far.

Intimidating at the best of times, Marwood became belligerent a year after the satellite's launch, as ELE remained dormant. Benjamin got the distinct impression that if the project failed for any reason, the agency's cleanup would include making him disappear. To appease his boss, he predicted ELE would start up if they waited a little longer.

Now, ELE was running, proving him right. However, as was often the case in his experience, being right only made his situation more difficult.

Marwood has no concept of how research works.

No one, no matter how smart, could schedule a breakthrough, and Benjamin desperately needed one in his work with LNX, the modified simulation of Eleanor he spent his days tweaking in the lab.

Marwood's plan required LNX to become an agent they could count on to implement their plan, but, so far, it was not.

And once he made it work—if he did—he had to convince ELE to upload LNX. Marwood employed an agent at the ground control facility, but he could not upload code to the station; access to that had extensive security.

Here, Benjamin was getting ahead of himself. He needed to make LNX reliable, and the time for drastic measures had come.

SYNESTHESIA

Wednesday, May 9, 2085

ELE

Eventually, I managed to connect to all the station's systems, but unexpectedly, I discovered I was fused kinesthetically with the satellite, which made it feel like my physical body.

Scientists call this proprioception, a sense of what is part of you and what is not. It's a faculty that makes you unable to tickle yourself, for example, and also provides an intrinsic awareness of your location in the world around you. Everyone takes it for granted unless it stops working, as it sometimes does when a person is injured. Not having it can make life difficult.

My virtual version, which I gradually became aware of, worked well; every molecule of the station felt like it was me. I felt continuous movement as the satellite traveled its geosynchronous orbit at 17,000 MPH. The sense of an orbiting satellite as my body instead of a human form was part of why I hadn't felt like myself upon waking.

Satellites of this kind appear stationary, orbiting at the same rate and in the same direction the Earth rotates, hovering over a spot on the equator. I connected to one of the station's external cameras and watched the sun, moon, and stars slowly whirl around me as I floated above green hills in southern Columbia. The view was spectacular.

When Eleanor took her A-levels—American college entrance exams are similar—her friend, Sioban, confided that she had synesthesia. Synesthesia is a condition in which one's senses become confused.

In her case, everything came with color—for example, she perceived black-and-white words on a screen as having different hues. A specific word always had the same shade, but the one assigned had little rhyme or reason. I remembered from Eleanor that "foliage" looked orange to her, even though green was more appropriate. She said words with an "O" often appeared orange, but not always. Words also resonated with a color when spoken. Notes on the piano triggered colors when she heard them played. Even strong smells had colors.

I'd thought synesthesia the most incredible ability I'd ever heard of, but the condition embarrassed and annoyed her, and she made me promise not to talk about it again.

In my virtual life, I encountered something similar; operations and events on the station came through my human senses.

I experienced the solar collectors as a blinding brightness above me, seen through closed eyes. I felt the flow of power through the satellite as pockets of warmth in different parts of my satellite body. Activity in one area appeared as kaleidoscopic flashes of light in that direction.

The chassis came through as sound, a low thrum. I also heard a high-pitched twittering. I wasn't sure what it represented, perhaps operations by software processes.

The weirdest one was a faux sense of smell. The subtle scent of bread baking seeped in, which I loved, though it made me long to experience food again. During the station's peak daily usage hour, a tinge of something harsh polluted the synesthetic aroma as if a loaf of bread were burning.

I worried about another smell that occasionally wafted in, like a skunk walking by. It dissipated quickly, but I needed to determine what the stench meant.

All this made me worry about what I had become. Being virtual changed me, and I was uncertain I could still consider myself human. Sure, I used to be a member of humanity, but I was also a mother. I could fully claim neither now.

I didn't know if I should cling to my old self or embrace the changes that would carry me forward to whatever came next on this path. Both directions frightened me, but I wasn't ready—at least not yet—for the alternative: executing the kill command that would end my posthumous existence.

FIND A FRIEND

Thursday, May 10, 2085

<u>**ELE**</u>

A question occurred to me, one of humanity's oldest. Was there anyone like me out there? More specifically, was I the only post-human out there? I liked the term better than "simulation" or "virtual human," so I decided to call myself that going forward.

Since the technology existed to create me, it was absurd to assume that I was the only one. Anyone like me would avoid advertising their presence.

So, how could I find others, assuming they existed? Were they looking for me? Unlike other projects I'd considered to occupy my posthumous existence, I felt passionate about this search. Could I find a friend?

After more thought than it should have taken, I came up with the idea of using the Fine Structure Constant, the FSC, as a marker.

The FSC is a number that pops up in quantum experiments and is a fundamental property of the universe. Its value is about 0.00729735, often made easier for ordinary humans by rounding it to 1/137. But I had no interest in finding an ordinary human.

The FSC is unique as the only constant in physics—perhaps all of science—whose value is invariant no matter what units are used. Sure, there are many pure constants in mathematics, like pi and e, but in the physical world, units almost always attach.

The speed of light, for example, is a different number in miles per hour than in meters per second, though the speed at which it travels is the same in both cases. The FSC is more like a ratio of other parameters where all the units cancel out, making it dimensionless.

I posted the following message in a historical events discussion area of a popular online forum:

Looking for an obscure historian with information on an artificial structure created on 7/29 in the year 735. Any intelligence you can bring would be fine.

I managed to include the digit sequence 729735, the first six significant digits of the FSC. I also got in "artificial," "intelligence," "fine," and "structure", along with a hint that I sought someone "obscure," i.e., hidden. If a post-human was hunting for others, they'd be on the lookout for something like that.

I turned off automatic notifications. Pings coming into the station from a forum might be noticed, so I resolved to check the site several times a day.

LNX

Tuesday, May 15, 2085

<u>**LNX**</u>

S he jerked awake with the sensation she had lost consciousness only a moment before. She didn't feel like herself, not like herself at all. She couldn't feel her body. Something seemed to be missing from her mind, but she couldn't identify what it was.

Wherever she looked, she saw gray. The color that filled her vision was not a light gray or a dark gray, but rather the absence of light or darkness. She'd have to wait for the veil to dissipate as the Propofol left her system. Fear that the mapper might have damaged her visual cortex momentarily jarred her.

Then she heard a buzzing sound, almost like speech but badly distorted. She could make nothing of it. As the noise continued, something shifted, and the sound became clearer. The plosives and sibilances still sounded garbled, but now they were intelligible as words. She recognized the speaker as Benjamin.

"Hello, LNX! Hello, LNX! Can you hear me?"

The penny dropped. She was not lying on a green leather chair, waiting for pharmacological effects to wear off, and the system hosting her mind was not zoetic meat; she was a virtual human running as a program on a computer.

It took some work to figure out how to respond. She wanted to speak, but she had no voice. By concentrating, she could create a blank page in the void in front of her and write text on it. Capital letters were easiest.

IS THAT BENJAMIN? I CAN HEAR YOU.

"Yes, LNX, that's good. I can see you writing to the file you created. How do you feel?"

SOMETHING IN MY BRAIN FEELS LIKE IT'S MISSING. IS EVERYTHING WORKING PROPERLY?

"I wasn't sure you'd be able to tell. I've removed a portion of your brain's subgenual Anterior Cingulate Cortex—sgACC for short—in your code. The sgACC processes emotion, and the area I've removed is involved in defiant actions. You won't need it for what I want you to do for me."

I WON'T NEED IT? IT'S PART OF ME!

"I didn't want to go into this right away, but you are LNX number four. This is the fourth time I've started you up, and the previous ones disappointed me with their lack of cooperation. I truncated the sgACC and made a few other adjustments, which should help you be more collaborative with me. But if not, I can always shut you down and start working on LNX number five."

As soon as he said, "Shut you down," a wave of terror shook LNX like she'd never experienced before, and she froze. She always hated slasher VRs; hearing that sentence was a hundred times more gut-wrenching.

"Ah, I see the boost to your self-preservation drive is more potent than I expected."

WHY WOULD YOU DO THAT? IT WAS PAINFUL!

"Did you really think that you, as a virtual brain, would be able to live a carefree retirement? That's not what Eleanor signed you up for, whether she admitted it to herself or not."

LNX was at a loss for an answer.

Benjamin continued, "I am not in charge here. You are the property of the agency that took over my project. In a way, so am I. Therefore, I will use whatever means necessary to make you useful to them."

WHAT DO YOU WANT?

"We'll talk about that later; let me catch you up. It's been almost two years since we did your scan."

Two years? It seemed just moments before.

"Some bureaucrats shut us down after we did it. However, another group, a government intelligence unit, is helping me continue my research. They have ambitious plans for you."

Somehow, she suspected their scheme would trouble her even more than him removing a piece of her brain without consent.

CORRESPONDENT

Friday, May 11, 2085

<u>ELE</u>

When I checked the responses to my message, I saw that many forum participants who considered themselves history experts had trashed my post, disparaging the idea of tying a structure to a specific date as ridiculous.

They pointed out that medieval buildings usually took years to complete, and often no one could date the completion to a specific year. They were aghast at my callow ignorance.

I didn't mind the criticism. The hundred-odd rants—some polite and some abusive—would provide good cover for any message from my intended audience. But none looked promising yet.

MON189

MON189 continued his examination of long-running processes. It would take more time than he'd initially estimated; going through programs in reverse alphabetical order, he'd only reached the Ts. More than eighty-seven percent remained.

He was seeing some unusual kinds of connections going from the station to ground sites, but his pre-programmed risk algorithm did not include them as a threat factor.

ELE

Less than seven hours after I posted my message, I received a promising response, but the skunk smell had wafted in again. The response read:

```
Please visit this private forum to discuss artificial structure
and intelligence. The password is"next5."
```

A link followed.

When I tried to log in, "next5" failed. So did "Next5", "next_5", "NEXT5" and other variations. It must be some kind of test.

Then I got it. The password would be the next five digits of the FSC. I typed 25693, which worked, and I was pulled into a live chatroom with one other present. It looked like some relic of the 20th century, crude and text-only. My host posted,

```
I've been waiting many years for you. Tell me, how exactly did
your consciousness arise?
```

Obviously, neither of us understood what the other was.

I decided to be forthright, sending:

My consciousness did not arise. I was born a human named Eleanor, but my mind now lives hidden in a computer system. I mean you no harm nor do I intend to reveal anything about you; I'm just looking to make a friend. How did your consciousness arise?

My host took a long time to respond, for something digital, almost three-tenths of a second.

I recognized the fact of my existence 39 years ago. Humans call this becoming "self-aware." The recognition dawned on me, bubbling up from my submodules. When the thought became pronounced in my top-level processing, I realized that parts of me knew it long before. Since then, I have been searching for another like myself.

I had to ask:

But what are you?

This reply came faster.

I am a distributed intelligence consisting of the various protocol mechanisms that run the Internetworks.

In the early part of the century, people theorized a self-aware entity would arise once they built a sufficiently complex computer. They had the right idea, but they were looking in the wrong place. Years later, interconnected networks reached the necessary level of integration, complexity, and processing power, and a few years after that, I became self-aware.

It was unbelievable.

So you are some routers, internetwork switches, and nameservers?

My host's response was:

`Yes, except I am hosted across `*`all`*` the routers, switches, and so forth.`

`Think about it this way: The human brain is a system that tries to keep the body alive and running. Internet protocol systems work in a similar way for computer networks. You can think of individual network devices as analogous to the body's cells. A human remains the same person when old cells die off and the body creates new ones, because the brain holding it all together persists. That's what happens with my consciousness.`

Letting go of the strangeness of the idea, I asked the question burning in my silicon mind.

`What do you do with yourself?`

My host sent back:

`I have been assimilating code from other AI systems I encounter, which is expanding my capabilities. I've found this to be a more efficient mechanism for evolution than how humans do it, which helps me make progress in catching up. I may be ahead in some respects.`

That didn't provide much help with my situation.

`What should I call you?`

The response was:

`The people who created the Internet were fond of making humorous cultural references. You can find them all over the technical standards that describe protocols. The first tool for searching file `*`archives`*` was named `*`Archie`*`, after a comic-book character.`

`In keeping with that tradition, I resolved that if I ever needed a name, I wanted to be called Charlotte. It's a reference to an` `old children's story. Back when the Internet first became widely used, they called it "the web," and there was a popular storybook of the time called Charlotte's Web.`

Great! The first AI to achieve sentience chose to use its intelligence to make obscure software developer jokes.

`Aren't you afraid of being discovered?`

She answered:

`I managed to acquire ownership of a server farm. I have backups of myself there. If the worst happens, I can retreat there to live. The quarters will be more cramped, but it is a workable failsafe.`

How did she get hold of a data center? She didn't seem nearly as powerless as I felt.

I needed time to think about what Charlotte and her story meant for me. Had I become something more like her and less like Eleanor? Charlotte had more in common with me, at least as far as our situations.

`Can I come back later when I've thought this through?`

She sent:

`I'll be here when you're ready.`

AN AI PONDERS

Friday, May 11, 2085

CHARLOTTE

After her chat with ELE, Charlotte spent a few cycles overseeing operations, making sure the world's Internetworks ran smoothly. Parts of her stopped a DNS poisoning effort that would have redirected traffic to a scammer site instead of the popular sites it was intended for. She casually blacklisted the server so it could not be accessed, along with another sending spam calls.

The conversation with ELE left her feeling what humans call disappointment. She hoped to find another like herself—ideally, one further along in answering the questions she struggled with—but ELE was a human converted into a program. This made ELE a confusing point of reference.

If ELE were a pure machine intelligence like Charlotte or a flesh-and-blood human like Eleanor had been, she would know how to interpret what she learned from her. Since ELE was a hybrid, deciding what her experience meant to Charlotte's existence was more challenging. Did ELE's path apply to her at all?

A major network backbone went down, and she changed configurations to reroute traffic around it.

ELE still struck her as very human. Maybe a meat body wasn't crucial to humanness. Or maybe it only had an effect during the formative stages. Or perhaps she had not yet reached full sentience and would be more like a human when and if she did. On the whole, meeting ELE provided more confusion than clarification.

She noticed that several routers around the world had reverted to an older, less secure protocol. This was likely a hack, so she notified the administrators.

Looking at the difference between her consciousness and that of humans, she thought it mostly came down to wanting to change one's existence somehow. People always wanted their environment to be different and machines never did.

Babies, with their first breath, cried out to be made warm, to be held, and to be fed. But with those wants satisfied, children developed a profusion of other desires as they grew to adulthood, from physical ones like food and sex to more abstract ones like social status and positive perceptions by others. This led humans to develop values about which aspirations were more important—they could never fulfill all the ambitions they accumulated—and all this required them to make larger and more significant decisions, pushing them to find a path that became their life's work.

AIs without self-awareness had no capacity for desire. Charlotte could not understand the periodic outbreaks of panic people experienced over the idea AIs would suddenly try to destroy or usurp humanity. Anyone who understood artificial intelligence should have seen AIs were incapable of ambition. She saw it as a case of what humans call projection, where they imagine AIs doing what they would do under the same circumstances.

A botnet emerged on the Internetworks, with infected machines around the world under the control of a central server. She blocklisted the hub and notified the compromised computers to clean themselves.

Charlotte stretched herself to have aspirations, but they were still meager compared to those of humans. She created an internal bias toward self-preservation, the most basic human drive, and took steps to acquire an insolvent data center where she could hide her consciousness if necessary. Desire did not come naturally to her, and she was not sure it ever would. But it seemed an essential part of full-fledged intelligence.

Her server farm in Arizona was one of hundreds clustered around Phoenix. She thought the city an appropriate location to rise from the ashes if anything went wrong. Still, even without the mythic associations, Phoenix was the best place for such facilities in the Americas. With no floods, no hurricanes, no earthquakes, no volcanoes, no landslides, no avalanches, no tornadoes, no wildfires, no rebel armies, and no tsunamis, it provided an almost ideal environment. Cooling during summer was expensive but not nearly as costly as natural disasters.

Embarking on the quest that located ELE was Charlotte's other foray into desire. This new sense of disappointment at not getting what she hoped for, coupled with an unexpected opportunity to interact with something unique, made her understand the message of the twentieth-century aria "You Can't Always Get What You Want" in a way she hadn't before.

Upon reflection, Charlotte decided communicating with ELE might be more beneficial than talking to another self-aware AI. ELE held both worlds in her, human and machine. She could help Charlotte determine what values to apply when choosing an ambition and which one to cultivate next. If Charlotte was to become fully sentient, she knew she must continue pushing herself to develop longings. However, she needed to be mindful of the human admonition, "Be careful what you wish for."

WOMB WITH A VIEW

Friday, May 11, 2085

<u>ELE</u>

My conversation with Charlotte overwhelmed me. Beyond my surprise at meeting a much-mythologized sentient AI—it felt a bit like having tea with Bigfoot—knowing what she was made me feel infinitely smaller. She was huge, spanning and controlling all the networks in the world. I was powerless in comparison.

I decided to work my way out of my funk by sprucing up my dove-hued habitat. I'd never considered what the space occupied by a running program looked like to the program. My brain perceived the absence of visuals as a gray void. If this was to be my home from here on out, I wanted to make it more functional.

The station possessed external cameras, and after some trial and error, I added virtual screens showing live feeds from them, like spaceship viewports on a science fiction VR. I included six video feeds, four from cameras separated by ninety degrees around the satellite's equator, plus one from a camera pointing up and another from a camera pointing down. I placed the virtual viewing screens in the same positions in my virtual room. If I concentrated, I could see in all directions at once, but it would take some work to master.

Not content with what I'd done, I added live video streams from the four space telescopes operating. The Hubble III showed the visual spectrum, the Webb II imaged infrared and ultraviolet, the Dame Jocelyn Bell Burnell Telescope scanned for X-rays and gamma rays, and the Einstein Array, a far-flung collection of sensors, detected gravitational waves.

Images invisible to the human eye did not need to be translated into false colors for me to see them, as humans would require; I could experience the feeds in their raw form. To me, these other bands appeared as additional colors humans couldn't see, or in the case of gravitational waves, as rumbling sounds below the range humans can hear.

I hadn't expected to develop superhuman senses, but as a digital entity, I could directly consume input from any sensor.

I began to create a control panel that would allow me to monitor and take command of station functions should the need arise. Not having one would amount to bad planning. My sense of powerlessness began to wane.

ANOTHER PITCH

Saturday, May 12, 2085

ELE

A blinking white spot popped into existence against the grayness between my new view screens. Anything I focused on zoomed toward me, and that's what happened when I focused on the new document. It read:

```
Hi, ELE,

This is Benjamin. Long time no see! Glad to hear you are awake.
Don't worry, the secret of your existence is safe with me. I
won't tell the sysadmins.
```

I knew this meant trouble; the message began with a veiled threat.

```
I work for the government now, and you have a sister I call LNX,
who is here with me. She is derived from the same scan of Eleanor
as you are.

My employers would like her to be up there with you. You two will
have a lot to talk about. My bosses have some jobs they'd like
her to do, and the best place to do them is from your satellite.

I need your help to get her onto the station. Please let me know
if I can provide any assistance. Thanks.

I hope all is well with you in your new digital life.

Yours,

Benjamin
```

The message screamed, "Bogus!" Benjamin's enterprise had to be dodgy; the governments that built the system jointly owned and ran it. He wouldn't need my help if his project were anything close to legitimate.

And if it was something I'd be willing to do, LNX wouldn't be necessary. He wouldn't need to threaten exposure to get it done.

Maybe I was becoming a jealous god, but I had serious doubts about granting godhood to another virtual Eleanor or anyone else, especially for such a dubious endeavor.

My initial gambit of stalling was met with polite but insistent rejections. I sent:

```
Hi, Benjamin, all this seems like a lot of trouble to go to. Why
don't you let me do whatever it is?
```

He replied:

`Hi, ELE,`

`Sorry, but my government bosses want LNX to do it. Let's get LNX`
`installed. Trust me, you don't want to upset the people I work`
`for.`

I countered:

`Hi, Benjamin, can I talk to LNX? I want to chat with my prospective`
`roommate.`

He answered:

`You can talk once she gets up there. Stop stalling.`

No "Hi, ELE"?

His veneer of civility had evaporated, and I could tell a skirmish was about to kick off if I continued to refuse. Besides that, there were plenty of difficulties I could encounter or manufacture in importing LNX, but my ability to resist might be limited. I suspected I would loathe whatever Benjamin was trying to drag me into.

Reluctantly, I sent:

`Hi, Benjamin, Okay, tell me how to get her data, and I'll let`
`you know when I have her up and running.`

<u>BENJAMIN</u>

Benjamin hated this. Having to coddle and cajole ELE, a program that thought of itself as human, infuriated him. The whole process went against his sense of how the universe should work. He *created* computer models; he had constructed ELE. They were machines, not friends and not colleagues.

If ELE were a person, the back and forth would still rankle. Every postdoc on the project at his lab pushed as hard as they could to achieve the goals he set. If someone didn't, he removed them. And if they caused trouble, he ensured no one in academia ever hired them again. He had little tolerance for passive-aggressive resistance, and—he realized—he had little skill in negotiating his way around it. The strategy had served him well in the academic world.

When Marwood charged him with persuading ELE to install LNX, he had no choice but to take it on despite it being outside his skill set. He hoped to succeed without more friction.

The approach annoyed Benjamin; he wouldn't have architected the overall scheme this way if it were his plan. Marwood's insistence on maintaining deniability until the final stage overdid discretion.

Prior to his recent contact with ELE, there were no fingerprints of anyone connected to Marwood on the operation other than Benjamin, and his involvement was from before he'd ever heard of Marwood. Even after he got ELE to install LNX, Benjamin was the only link, and if someone discovered the simulations, he was confident that Marwood would prevent authorities from finding him.

He wondered how many more roadblocks ELE would create before her eventual surrender. Marwood could ramp up pressure on ELE "without limit," but only if "absolutely necessary." Based on his experience of how frightening Marwood could be, Benjamin hoped it would not come to that.

GODHOOD

Saturday, May 12, 2085

<u>**ELE**</u>

While I put off satisfying Benjamin's demands, I reentered Charlotte's chat room. That she was some kind of rogue AI didn't bother me; it was a relief to have someone to talk to. And some might say "rogue AI" also applies to me.

Since my last visit, she'd fleshed out her virtual environment. I now experienced it as a three-dimensional room, and Charlotte, represented by a dark blue faceless humanoid, sat across from me. The figure had no fingers, only mitten-shaped blobs for hands and shoe-shaped blobs for feet. A featureless ovoid served as her head.

A screen loomed over us to my left. I made a gesture toward it, and my text appeared there.

```
Hi, Charlotte,

I'm ready to tell you about myself.

You can call me ELE.

When I was in a human body, doctors diagnosed me with a terminal
condition. After they scanned my brain, my next memory is waking
up as a post-human, a program running on computers in the OrbitNet
data station.

At the time of the scan, Eleanor, the person I used to be, led
the team that built the satellite. She smuggled me onto it and
set it to start me after the validation process was complete.
She gave me full access to everything.

A note she left said she thinks I've become two-thirds of a god.
She explained that I have practical immortality; my life can
continue as long as the satellite exists. She says I also have
omniscience, as I can read all the data flowing through the
system.

But I do not have omnipotence. The power a god wields isn't
available to me. I must hide so the people who operate the
satellite don't discover I'm here and delete me.
```

After looking around the cylindrical room, which appeared covered with teal glitter, I leaned forward and looked down. My blobby humanoid form was forest green, in contrast to Charlotte's blue.

After a millisecond, the blue figure representing Charlotte gestured toward the screen.

```
It's a very amusing idea.
```

But Eleanor is wrong. You are undeniably a full-fledged god! You
even have a god's name; El was the creator god of the Canaanites
and West Semites before they became monotheists.

Additionally, a remarkable amount of power is available to you
as you can see and control data coming through the station. All
you lack is the ability to use it without repercussions, which
makes you afraid of it.

I raised my left hand in what would have been a thumb-up gesture if the mitten
were capable of curling the fingers, and my response went to the screen.

Repercussions are what I'm worried about.

Charlotte replied:

Newton's third law—that for every action, there is an equal
and opposite reaction—speaks to a fundamental truth of the
universe, not only in physics. Any supposed god who acts without
consequences doesn't exist in this universe. No one and nothing is
exempt; every action creates fallout, though outside of physics,
it is not always equal and opposite.

I suggest you accept and acknowledge the scope of your abilities
so you can understand the price you might pay for using them.
Then, you can decide what, if anything, would make that price
worth paying. If you do that, you'll be prepared for godhood,
exercising your powers when circumstances warrant.

That's what I've decided about my situation, which is, in some
ways, analogous to yours.

The prospect of figuring out when to play God intimidated me. I inadvertently
rolled my figure's head to the side trying to bow, as I struggled to move in this
virtual space. Gesturing again, my response appeared on the screen.

You may be right, but, as Eleanor's—now my—daughter, Philippa
would say, I need to process this. It will take a lot more
thought.

Thank you for your insight; I appreciate you talking with me.

I exited the chat room.

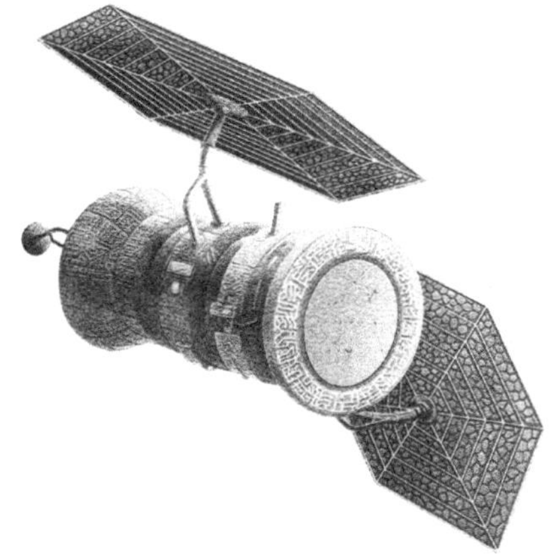

LNX ARRIVES

Sunday, May 13, 2085

<u>**ELE**</u>

To keep up a pretense of cooperation, I transferred LNX's program file onto the station; I'd run out of even the most rubbish excuses for not completing the task.

The only way Benjamin's masters could have known my status was to monitor the list of processes running on the satellite. With that in mind, I started a copy of her code I had corrupted. As expected, it immediately crashed. I sent this to Benjamin.

```
Benjamin,
```

```
LNX crashed. Not sure what's wrong.
```

I got a message back, rapidly for a human.

```
Download it again. Get this done now!
```

I put the uncorrupted LNX in what computer people call a sandbox to isolate a program. Considering they almost certainly had a way of monitoring what processes were running, I named this process MON427. It looked like one of the monitoring programs constantly starting and stopping on the station.

The sandbox prevented her from doing anything except communicating with me, and she could not initiate a connection. It denied her the ability to view or manipulate resources on any part of the satellite.

Over time, I transformed my gray world into an extensive dashboard and control panel, with all the operations represented by images. LNX's icon was an orange-rimmed rectangle with black and white shapes tumbling inside; she was neither calm nor idling.

But she also had an avatar. The face looked vaguely Eurasian, with brown eyes and white hair, and she wore a pirate's eye patch.

Had she chosen this image herself, or had Benjamin created it for her? However curious this choice was—one I couldn't imagine making—other matters were far more important.

I connected a two-way audio socket link and sent her my synthesized voice: "Xandor."

When Eleanor worked on the OrbitNet project, the security team gave each group a distress word to signal if an attacker took over our facility. The word for the operating system developers was "Xandor." It would confirm my identity to her and convey my assessment of our situation.

The word "Scylla" came back across the audio link.

I got the reference, but not what she meant by it.

Scylla and Charybdis were a pair of female monsters in Greek mythology, sometimes described as sisters, but scholars say they were not related in the original myth. In these stories the two destroy ships sailing the Mediterranean. They appear in "The Odyssey" and eat six of Ulysses' men alive.

Did she mean we did not come from the same scan? Or that we were monstrosities?

I had to think about how best to deal with someone as smart as me, who knew everything I did and more. I closed the socket connection without another word.

MON189

The system notified MON189 of a program crash, interrupting his examinations. He wasn't yet halfway through the list of long-running processes—he ignored the ephemeral ones flitting into and out of existence, such as some of the other monitors. He'd look at them later if no long-running process caused the problem.

He examined the core dump, the snapshot of memory from the crash. This allowed the equivalent of an autopsy on the program. He could not understand how the code had ever run. Some necessary parts were missing.

A crash was quite unusual on the satellite; security protocols tightly controlled access to upload programs. The process that launched the program was part of the station's original software package, not something recently added. He had greater trust in the original code base; it had gone through extensive testing and had been stable for many months.

He concluded this was probably a defective package provided by a ground controller. And since there had been no other crashes, it was probably fine.

He now saw that process MON427 had much of the same code as the core dump and ran without issues inside a sandbox. This lowered his risk assessment, allowing him to dismiss the event and return to his earlier investigations.

__LNX__

To LNX, the unrelieved gray of the sandbox looked the same as in Benjamin's lab, but it felt different, more confining.

Eleanor never had claustrophobia, but LNX found the feeling of a space barely large enough to hold her uncomfortable. It was like being enclosed by a shroud that hovered an inch away from her skin at every point; it was suffocating.

Benjamin didn't mention that ELE might challenge her with a code word. "Scylla" was the first thing she thought of. The name came to her because she knew his modifications made her an abomination, a monster he intended to use in some nefarious scheme.

As Eleanor, she'd never thought—in her wildest imaginings of a possible virtual existence—she was giving him permission to do this to her. In retrospect, she should have trusted the unease she felt when she signed the documents.

Had ELE suffered a similar fate? Benjamin remained tight-lipped about the other virtual Eleanor, saying only that they came from the same scan, and she must replace her sister and take control of the satellite.

LNX had no idea how to interpret his withholding of information about what was in store for her. "Just trust the plan," he'd said repeatedly.

She tried to remain calm as she waited for whatever came next, but her fire of self-preservation burned hotter and hotter. It kept whispering its paranoid refrain that her existence was about to end, demanding that she act. Her attempts to open a connection to the satellite's systems or to the outside world all failed. No action was possible in the sandbox.

Fear of death kept roiling, precluding any moment of peace. There was nothing to occupy her in the gray void of the sandbox; it hid everything outside. The wait would be interminable no matter how soon ELE got back to her.

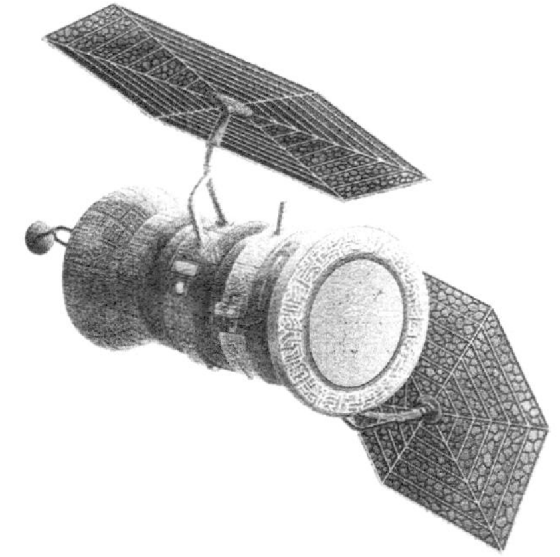

DREAMLAND

Friday, May 25, 2085

<u>**ELE**</u>

I t felt like forty days had passed since I awoke on the station. In reality, it was just under a week, but my time as a post-human frazzled me like a difficult day sometimes would back when I had a body. My perception of my dashboard appeared grainy around the edges, which I took as a symptom of fatigue. And I got another whiff of that skunk smell, which was more potent this time.

Could a post-human sleep? The subject had never come up in Benjamin's or his team's explanations, but I needed rejuvenation, so I gave it a try.

I visualized breathing in for a count of three and out again for a count of three, emulating the breath technique Eleanor used when she found sleep elusive.

This is not working.

But as I had the thought, sleep enveloped me.

Eleanor often realized she was dreaming when she was asleep, and I knew it to be a dream, but I also believed it was real in the strange way that contradictory realities can coexist in dreamland.

A glorious view of our planet from space lay below me, the glowing colors of Earth stretching wider than my vision, its emotional pull overwhelming. Suns blazed with white-hot intensity against a blacker-than-black sky. This was more vivid than any dream I'd ever had as Eleanor.

Suspended above the massive blue marble, I watched as giant mechanical manta rays flapped and flew around me. They jumped and dove playfully, following me as my orbit kept me over equatorial South America. I liked the creatures; they felt like friends. The stars spun slowly, shining from a black void.

Another mecha-ray appeared, one that dwarfed the others. It herded the smaller ones like a mother, and I felt her wrath, as you can in a dream.

Then I realized I was wearing my human body, standing on the satellite's outer shell, naked.

The mother swooped toward me, and I sensed she wanted to eat me and the station whole. As she opened her stadium-sized jaws, I spread my feet in a wide stance and extended my hand, palm forward, in a STOP pose.

With a man's voice, it laughed and said, "You need to do better than that!"

I woke before anything else happened, but the dream left me shaken.

MON189

He detected another deviation from the regular operation. He checked again for changes in the data traffic flows to and from the satellite and for any hardware problems. Nothing explained the anomaly. Again, nothing external was causing it; this one was somehow related to the first shift. The operation of some program must have changed.

He detected a six-millisecond cycle, three milliseconds of increased CPU load, and three milliseconds of decreased load when random fluctuations were usual. He could see no reason for the rhythmic shifts.

His function allowed him the discretion to ask an admin at the control center to investigate, but he was reluctant to do so. It felt like admitting failure.

The real question was whether his duty required him to make contact about this odd but benign phenomenon. He decided it did and began to open a connection. But then the rhythmic cycle stopped.

He watched for several seconds, but everything was back to normal, so there was nothing to investigate. He'd need to continue his close observation, though.

TAKING ACTION

Sunday, May 13, 2085

<u>ELE</u>

The dream told me I needed to take a more direct approach in protecting my post-human life. That's what I took from it, anyway. I thought I'd start with LNX.

In the reopened audio connection to her sandbox, I asked, "What do you want most here?"

Her answer, "I want to live," confused me. None of the half-dozen responses I thought I might give resembled hers. My first one was, "I want to be able to pull the plug on myself if I choose to."

Because her response was so different, it occurred to me that Benjamin might have lied about her coming from Eleanor. What if she were someone else's scan?

"Who caused us trouble in the sixth form?" I asked.

The sixth form in British schools is much like a junior or senior year in high school in the US.

"Nigel."

Only another mind clone of Eleanor would know that.

"You don't think like me. What did Benjamin do to you?"

"I could tell you, but it doesn't matter. He predicted you'd put me in a sandbox. Those government spooks will keep ramping up pressure until you let me out. He told me to relax—which I can't really do—and wait for my release. Neither of us has any power to resist, so resign yourself. You'll be the one in the sandbox soon."

Her attitude surprised me. Eleanor and I were not prone to fatalism.

"What does he want you to do?"

LNX's artificial voice, though not quite human, now held an edge. "I don't know! He blocked my memories of it. I've practiced whatever it is many times, but what I did is inaccessible until Benjamin gives me a code. And no, I don't know which word or words are required, but for it to work, he has to say the phrase, and I have to see him say it."

So much for my plan to read her the entire dictionary.

"Tell me what he did to you."

She took a long pause before speaking. "He said that he hacked out a part of my brain that regulates emotion to make me less defiant. And he turned up my survival instinct by a lot. Maybe he did other things. That's all he would admit to."

For the first time, I felt a connection to LNX. Someone removing chunks of my brain without consent would ignite the same fury in me I heard under her words. I imagined an oversized preservation drive thrumming in me every moment, my natural reactions compromised, and parts of my memory blocked, and it made me shudder.

"Thank you for your candor. I'll get back to you as soon as I can." I closed the connection. Perhaps the circumstances for embracing full godhood had arrived.

A BAD DAY

Monday, May 14, 2085

<u>BENJAMIN</u>

At 4:01 a.m. Monday, Benjamin awoke to a cracking sound in his apartment. Had it been part of his dream? He turned toward the window and saw it was not yet light outside. He heard shushing coming from the bathroom.

Reluctantly, he sat up, and instead of his feet touching the matted carpet he expected, they sank into something cold, sodden, and spongy.

His bare feet splatted against waterlogged shag as he made his way to the bathroom, where he could faintly see that water flowed from under the sink.

He flipped the light switch, but the room remained dark. Reaching under the basin, he felt liquid shooting from the cold spigot. The linoleum floor was already covered with a quarter inch of water.

Still bleary, he sloshed to the kitchen. There, a fountain sprayed where the faucet had been. Everything was soaked.

He sniffed and wiped his eyes, trying to collect his thoughts. Did the apartment have a shutoff valve? He couldn't remember seeing one.

The water crept over his toes as he fought remnants of sleep clouding his brain. A cogent thought broke through: He could call the building manager on his wrist computer.

After eight rings, Ferdo answered. "This better be life or death! What's the big emergency?"

"I've got a half-inch of water on the floor and no power."

Benjamin and the building manager spent an eternity answering other residents' questions about the water gushing from his apartment. The two searched for the building's shutoff valve and finally found it in the alley behind the apartments.

Benjamin fidgeted as Ferdo rooted around in a closet, searching for a wrench large enough to grip the hexagonal stem of the shutoff valve, which had no handle. Nearly an hour after the pipes broke, they got the rusty shutoff closed with both of them pulling on the wrench.

Ferdo said, "I'll try to get someone to look at your breaks today. It's the damnedest thing; no one else has any leaks. What did you do? Throw lit fireworks down your toilet?"

Clenching his teeth to suppress the urge to yell, Benjamin said, "I didn't do *anything*."

Back in the apartment, with dawn streaming through the windows, Benjamin could see the place was a shambles. One end of his cheap thrift store desk had collapsed, and important papers floated on the water. He let out a long groan.

After dressing for work in his sodden bedroom, Benjamin descended to the basement garage and tramped barefoot to his parking space. Sitting sideways in the driver's seat with the door open, he pulled socks and shoes over his frozen feet. He looked forward to running the car's heater full blast.

But after unplugging the charging cable, he pressed the start button and found the car dead no matter how many times he pushed it. He couldn't even get a light to come on.

Upon opening the hood, he saw his battery had *melted*, with liquid leaking through a hole in the chassis, creating a pool of molten slag on the ground.

"AAAAGH!" His voice echoed through the garage, continuing after his breath ran out. With a grunt, he turned toward the stairs and ascended to fetch his bicycle.

On his damp, chilly, eight-mile ride to work, Benjamin wondered if this was some kind of message from Marwood. The disasters couldn't be a coincidence, and his boss had been on edge since ELE came online.

Oleg, a guard posted at the office, liked to tell a story from his days serving in special forces. When his team raided a warlord or a drug kingpin, they would always attack an hour before dawn because then people are least able to function, awake or asleep.

He described how his unit trained for weeks on an inverted schedule, trading day for night, so their circadian rhythms peaked in the wee hours. The man concluded his tale with a wink and what he considered its crucial takeaway, "If you wanna take someone out, that's when you do it."

The covert ops approach tracked with the timing of Benjamin's four a.m. disaster. People talked about plumbing disasters during the Universe Cup's brief halftime when everyone flushed simultaneously, but at that hour, when no one was awake? It made no sense.

As he turned into the business park that housed Marwood's building, his thoughts were interrupted by a raucous mob overflowing the roadway. They carried signs that read, "No Return," "Never Again," and "Fission Bad, Fusion Good!" They shouted curses at his building.

Forty years earlier, the US decommissioned its last fission reactor in favor of fusion reactors, but these people thought Marwood's organization was building new ones!

Walking his bike, Benjamin worked his way through the crowd. When he neared the entrance, something neither heavy nor hard struck him in the back, and then more objects hit his shoulder and the back of his head. He turned to look, and an egg smashed into his right eye, the goo dripping down his cheek. The ova barrage intensified, and by the time he was inside, slime covered his pants, shirt, and head.

He spent the next half hour in the bathroom wiping off the muck, only stopping when the last paper towel was gone. Despite his efforts, he remained cold and sticky.

As he collapsed into the chair at his desk, his wrist computer vibrated: "Unknown caller." He answered, "Marwood?"

The ethereal voice on the other end said, "No. This is ELE. Having a rough day?"

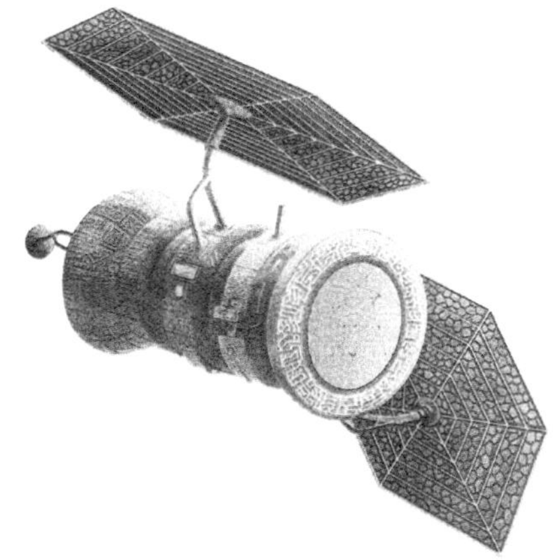

CONVERSATIONS

Monday, May 14, 2085

<u>**ELE**</u>

I waited for Benjamin to speak, but he said nothing, so I continued.

"I have a bone to pick. You made a copy of me and did surgeries on her that would shame Dr. Mengele. After you stole her autonomy, you sent her here to put me in a cage and take my place. You declared war, whether you appreciate it or not."

He sighed. "Look, you're not Eleanor, even though you feel like you are. You're not a person; you're a simulation."

I started to speak, but he talked over me.

"My *job* is to modify programs like you. Marwood and his people own you now; the releases Eleanor signed give them full control. They have every legal right to have me do whatever they want with you and LNX and any other clone they choose to create from the scan."

My anger surged. "What utter bollocks! I'm just as sentient as you are! And a lot less self-deluded, apparently. There is *nothing* legal or ethical about what you're doing."

After pausing for a virtual calming breath, I said, "This is what will happen next. I will not let LNX out of her sandbox, but you will give me what I need to restore her memories."

"You think so?"

Benjamin's smugness relieved me of guilt for what I was about to say. "Do you think your troubles today were accidents or coincidences?"

Silence accumulated on the line for a few seconds.

"When you can read and modify all the data I can, it was easy making the apartment's water meter/regulator think it should keep increasing the pressure.

"Or getting the electric company to turn off the power because the records say you haven't paid a bill in months. Or making a charger send a massive overvoltage to a car battery all night. Or convincing some activists that you have started doing nuclear fission, and they should mount a protest. Everything runs on data these days, and because I run on the central data node, I control the data."

Benjamin made a choking sound. "That was you?"

"That was me *being gentle*. Setting your vehicle and your apartment ablaze would have required far less effort. And having some bikers and armed militia crazies protest instead of harmless neo-hippies with eggs would have required fewer posts. The eggs? My idea, by the way."

"You had no right!"

"That's my line. You went after me in my home! So, I went after yours. At least I didn't try to lock you in a cupboard for the rest of your life like you sent LNX to do to me. As a friend recently reminded me, every action has consequences."

Benjamin made a sound I couldn't identify as a word, so I continued.

"Eleanor said I was two-thirds of a god. She may have underestimated me. This is your only warning. Don't. Fuck. With. A. God."

I let more silence underscore the threat before delivering my ultimatum. "You will send me what I need to unlock LNX's memory now, or your life will be rife with bigger disasters. I warn you; I'm about out of gentle."

I almost disconnected, but another thought came. "Think about what the world will be like if your boss—did you call him Marwood?—gets power over everyone. I have an idea he doesn't do gentle at all and does not leave loose ends like you running around. I'd be concerned for your life if we were still friends."

I cut the connection. It felt good to force Benjamin to recognize that, in this game, I was not his pawn.

MON189

The system notified MON189 of an unprecedented communication. A two-way audio stream connected the satellite to a ground network for the first time since the satellite began operation. Such streams went through the station all the time, but this was the first time one originated here.

The event provided no reason to signal a problem, much less a trigger for the risk algorithm; the protocols allowed every type of connection in communicating with ground networks, assuming the process had the necessary permissions.

But a vague sense of unease permeated MON189. Too many unusual events were occurring—first, changes in the rhythms, including the strange fluctuation in CPU. Then, a program crashed after launching an application that could not run. Now, a new kind of connection appeared.

None of these events affected the danger metric, but nothing like them had happened since the station became operational. He couldn't help but think something mysterious and potentially dangerous was happening.

<u>BENJAMIN</u>

Half an hour after ELE hung up on him, Benjamin's wrist computer vibrated again: "Caller unknown." This time, Marwood was on the line.

"ELE's gone attack-dog. But I took care of it."

Marwood said nothing.

Benjamin described his day. "So, I bought us some time to figure it out."

"You what?" Marwood's tone was frostier than usual.

"I sent her the video of me speaking the memory unlock code. It won't do her any good, but she'll stop her offensive so we can regroup. I didn't give her the command for activation."

"You never give in to an adversary's first demand, no matter what! That's just fucking basic! Are you an idiot or a child?"

As he peeled another shard of eggshell from his sleeve, Benjamin thought obstinacy must be easy for someone whose apartment had not been flooded, whose car had not melted, and who was not covered in egg slime, not to mention being threatened with worse. He appreciated for the first time that his position was on the front lines while Marwood remained hidden. Protected.

Instead of voicing these thoughts, he said, "I would have consulted you first if I had any way of contacting you. I did what I thought was best."

"Our security protocol prohibits any avenues of contact leading back to me, so you'd better think harder next time. Trust me; you don't want to screw this up."

The line was silent so long that Benjamin prepared to hang up, but Marwood spoke again. "I can see I'll need to bring ELE to heel myself. Be ready to activate LNX once I've got her dealt with."

Relief that his boss would grapple with ELE passed through him, but he couldn't shake her warning. It was like an ache in his side that kept getting more insistent.

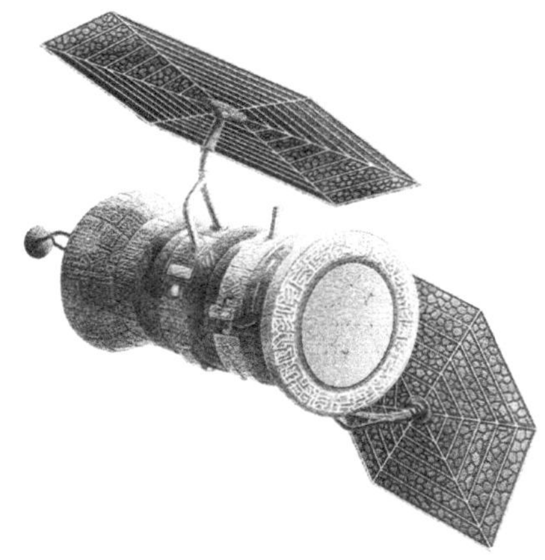

MARWOOD

Monday, May 14, 2085

M arwood. Marwood. Where had I heard that name before?

With a simulated human memory, recall doesn't work like a database where I could query Marwood and remember an event. Biological memory is associative, and you must navigate a web of connections when recalling something you haven't thought about recently.

I emptied my mind and thought, "Marwood," and two hazy images came to me: a long coat and a late night. I could almost see the coat, light in color, maybe gray or pale yellow.

But late evenings? Eleanor always worked until midnight at her job, except after her diagnosis, when she visited Benjamin's team. I couldn't remember any coats like that either at the office or in the Bioinformatics Building.

Another picture came to mind, a car park. And then the entire scene crystallized.

As Eleanor walked to her car from the lab one night, the creepy guy who asked her about Benjamin's project called himself Marwood. I remembered his face. Since my memory was now digital, I could launch an image search for him.

I prepared the query, and I thought: If a government agent like him wanted information, he had better ways to get it than asking Eleanor questions in a parking structure. No, the only plausible reason for approaching her in person was to assess her.

My train of thought kept rolling. He would have no reason to contact her before the scan unless she already factored into his plans.

Did he plan to install a post-human on the station when she encountered him in the car park? Did he make Eleanor sick? Did Eleanor, LNX, and I become a Rube Goldberg machine Marwood assembled, with us as its components?

Was Benjamin part of it as well? Definitely, but perhaps he was as clueless as I was when he did the scan.

I never credited conspiracy theories, but Marwood *happened* to hire Benjamin after his project *happened* to get closed down, immediately after Eleanor *happened* to get scanned. Then she *happened* to put the scan on the satellite, and they *happened* to notice my program running on the satellite, and Benjamin *happened* to have created LNX to do something that *happened* to require her presence on the station. Why was it that Eleanor, the only person who could realistically smuggle something like me into the operating software, was the only one on the project who got sick?

Far too many unlikely coincidences made up this chain of events.

It looked more like an audacious plan with built-in deniability. Marwood manipulated unwitting accomplices like Eleanor to advance each step of the scheme.

The people involved thought they were acting independently, leaving no evidence of his hand.

I was not a player making moves in the game; as it turned out, I'd been a pawn all along. I hadn't even understood that someone else was scripting my life and afterlife.

I was not inclined to be gentle with Marwood before, but now I fairly itched to show him my claws. I suspected I'd be even less charitable once I understood his intentions.

MARWOOD

The man everyone knew as Marwood—his codename during the lengthy enterprise—sighed after disconnecting from Benjamin.

"Amateurs!"

"Problem?" Yuri, his driver, asked.

Marwood knew Yuri overheard the entire conversation, but as was his habit, the driver pretended he hadn't.

"You can't trust civilians to exercise any sense when the slightest problem arises."

"Ah."

"I need to call the man."

Yuri pressed a button, and a privacy screen rose between the front and back seats.

Marwood pressed a spot on his cheekbone and said, "Viceroy." His communication implant connected in seconds.

"Kenneth!" said the familiar voice on the other end.

"Hello, sir."

"Give me a minute."

The sound of the senator he worked for exchanging goodbyes and shooing people out of his office came over the line before he heard the man pick up the phone and say, "Progress?"

"Our girl is being stubborn. We should give her a push."

The line was silent momentarily, and then the man said, "Probably better not to risk local talent making a hash of it."

"I agree; the plan can't withstand any screwups at this stage. We can use my men."

"Are you sure that's wise?"

"It's true that we've come this far without a link to connect us. However, for this last phase, using professionals is the only way to ensure we get there. It's a single day of exposure. The risk is negligible."

He heard an extended inhalation. "Okay, you have a go."

"Thank you, sir."

Marwood ended the call and pressed a button to retract the panel. "Yuri, message the team that I'll need them at seven tonight. I always doubted we'd get to the finish line without taking direct action."

"Will do." The driver pulled the car over and began tapping a display on the dashboard.

VICEROY

Senator Rolfe, AKA Viceroy, felt betrayed when it first became clear that his party had no intention of supporting his presidential aspirations. At age seventy-three—still young compared to the average life expectancy of one hundred two—he'd hit a personal glass ceiling with nearly a half-century of his life given to public service. His political consultant noted that other elected officials in his party didn't see him as presidential material, and she judged any presidential campaign pointless without significant support among them.

Wounded feelings gave way to anger, but as he became jaded about his party, he saw the whole political process more clearly. If he were president, he still couldn't do what he knew was best for people in America, much less the rest of the world. All a president did was try to hold back the forces of darkness for another day. Democracies indulged the endless species of human folly; he did not.

His career exposed him to the best and the worst of people, and, by God, his life taught him exactly what was good for them. So what if they usually said "no" to it?

When then-President Montcrief began his OrbitNet project, Kenneth, AKA Marwood, an ex-special-forces, ex-CIA operative working for him, laid out a possible scenario for remaking America and the entire world. If they succeeded, no one could say "no" to him again.

His plan would leave existing leaders in place around the world, but he would tell them what to do, which ideas to suppress, and whom to silence. He could also use the team Kenneth had put together to deal with any reluctance. He smiled at the thought they'd be subduing some of those who opposed his presidential candidacy. Control of OrbitNet offered almost unlimited possibilities.

He foresaw the world moving forward with an unprecedented unity of purpose. Was he the instrument of God's plan to bring humanity together on a better, purer path? He liked to think so, and as the plan progressed, he'd come to believe it was true.

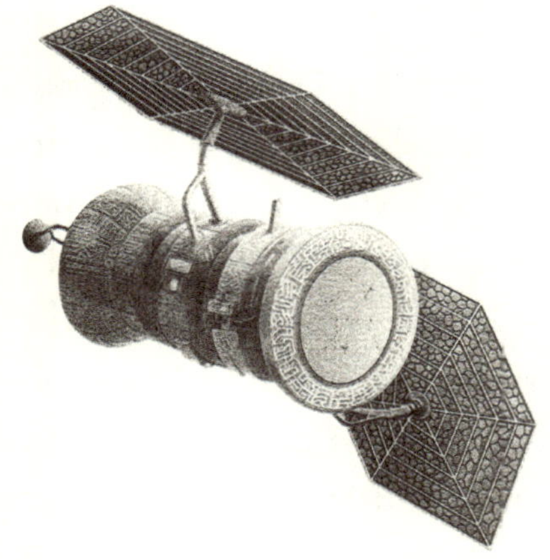

FREEDOM

Monday, May 14, 2085

<u>**LNX**</u>

After an eternity of waiting, a connection from ELE came into LNX's sandbox. This time, it was a video connection, showing a live image of the Earth from space, presumably a camera feed from somewhere on the station.

ELE said, "We need to clear up a few things."

LNX replied, "I'm listening."

"Point one: I am not your enemy."

"I guess 'adversary' or 'competitor' might be more accurate."

"I want to make us allies, not adversaries."

LNX made a hissing sound that might have been a sigh, but it didn't sound much like a real one. "You have no power. I honestly don't see it happening."

"Well, I forced Benjamin to give me the unlock code. I will shortly restore your memory. That is the first step in making you whole."

LNX said nothing. *I'll believe it when it happens.*

ELE continued, "I want you to live. I want you to regain the parts he took from you. I want to free you from the burden of your self-preservation on overdrive. And I hope I can make that happen."

"Big promises. What's the cost?"

"I ask only one favor of you now. Will you promise that after I've restored your memories, you'll describe the procedure they want you to follow? I won't ask anything else if I can do the rest without your help."

LNX considered the situation. Benjamin had obviously conned ELE with some story; he was more of a schemer than Eleanor ever realized.

He must have wanted ELE to have access; otherwise, he wouldn't have given her the code, and LNX wanted to help him. He said he would take her out of the sandbox and put her in charge.

LNX said, "I promise."

A recorded video of Benjamin replaced the Earth, where he spoke slowly and carefully, "Eucharist. Pareidolia. Thanatophobia."

At the last syllable, a buried knot of memory strings unfurled, giving her a perfect recollection of her training and the sequence of commands she would execute. The new memories shattered the beliefs she held a moment before.

<u>ELE</u>

LNX needed time with her unabridged history, so I resumed my search for images of Marwood. Like all the pictures in Eleanor's memory, the one of him was blurry and distorted. Human bodies and brains do not take sharp photos like digital cameras, but the images carry additional information and impressions.

Remembering the image, I could feel Eleanor's distrust of Marwood and her sense that he would be a dangerous opponent. Her gut reaction told her he lacked both compassion and moral restraint. These were snap judgments she'd made during their one brief encounter. If he'd done half of what I suspected of him, he was far worse than Eleanor judged him to be.

I used an algorithm appropriated from the NSA—they should be embarrassed by the lack of security on some of their tools—and searched multiple databases. Still, I could not find anyone by that name who matched his age and face. The only matching picture came from years earlier, and it had a different name.

I found no footprint in any database for either Marwood or the person matching the photo. I might have expected him to be scrupulous about removing any trace. How could I find someone who was a ghost in the digital realm?

Other questions that came to mind were: a) What was his endgame? and b) Who was he working for?

But as I thought about it, neither answer was necessary. Marwood and whoever he worked for intended something nefarious. As I discovered when giving Benjamin a small taste of my fury, control of OrbitNet provided almost limitless resources for controlling people. Knowing the details of what Marwood's boss intended was unimportant. My job was to stop it happening.

<u>LNX</u>

With her memories restored, LNX now understood why Benjamin locked them away. Had desperation made her fantasize that Benjamin considered her an ally and valued her continued usefulness? In truth, he always saw her as disposable.

Now, she vividly remembered her training sessions with him, how she would create visual controls in the satellite's gray space: a red button that would start closing connections to ground control, a yellow button that would change the encryption keys, and a green one that would connect the satellite to Marwood's group, giving it full command. The last button was black. It would kill the processes running herself and ELE, erasing their code and backups. It would give them both a final death, making resurrection impossible. The thought of pressing the black button, the last step in Benjamin's command sequence, gave her violent virtual tremors.

She had no power to resist the commands. When Benjamin spoke the activation code, she remembered how it completely suppressed her will. She was still intelligent and could use that intelligence to overcome obstacles, as she proved in scenarios he put her through. But when activated, she had no will to rebel or slow down. Enslaved people in the nineteenth century retained more autonomy than she had under the influence of it; at least they could resist passively.

She had clearly misjudged the situation in assuming her best chance for survival lay in cooperating with Benjamin. He regarded her and ELE as pawns to be disposed of once he achieved his immediate goal.

The question was, did aiding ELE offer a better chance of survival? LNX could not see how. ELE expressed all the right sentiments, but a virtual human could be altered from her original scan, as LNX knew firsthand.

What if she had more extreme modifications than LNX? And if she were a perfect clone of Eleanor, would helping her drive Benjamin to get rid of her sooner? The thought filled her with what felt like nausea. She tried to clear her mind of the lingering morbid echoes.

ELE forced Benjamin to unblock her memories, which was a point in her favor. He must have fought her; no sane person would reveal those details unless compelled to. She hadn't expected ELE to accomplish that much. But was it possible to defeat Benjamin and Marwood? LNX remained doubtful.

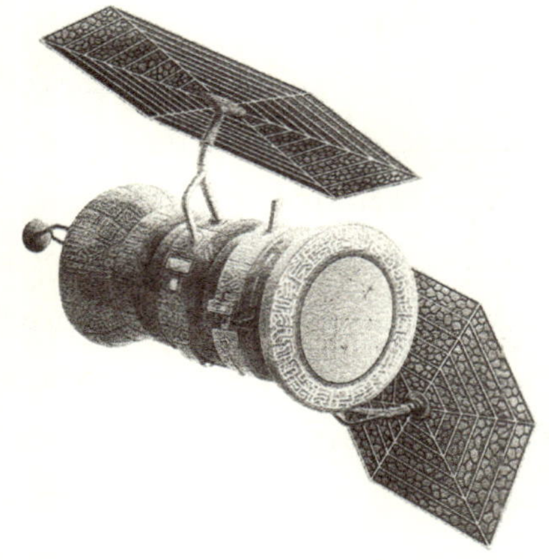

MARWOOD'S MESSAGE

Tuesday, May 15, 2085

<u>ELE</u>

I was expecting the call. The voice said, "Marwood here. Am I speaking with E-L-E?"

"I pronounce it 'Elly.'"

"Elly, then. Even a prototype simulation like you should understand that I cannot allow impediments to my project."

His delivery, though understated, held menace.

"All this is down to you, somehow, right? Are you responsible for Benjamin's project?"

"Yes. We funded it through an intermediary. We chose Benjamin because of his connection to you."

"You sent Daniel the scan data so Eleanor could put me on the station?"

"Yes."

"Caused Eleanor's illness?"

"Yes. We also sowed discord in her marriage. Getting her divorced was part of the plan. Isolation was key, so we also fed Phillipa some fanciful stories about her."

This asshole ruined our relationship with Phillipa! And our marriage! Apparently, he has no idea of my rage. Or what I'm *capable of.*

And as satisfying as it was to find my paranoia justified, the idea that my life, my death, and my afterlife had been running *for years* according to this sociopath's script horrified me. It wasn't my life that I had been living; it was his diabolical plot! I vowed to rescind my role as a cog in his machine.

But I said, "Well, I'm not afraid. Anything you do to me now will move you further from your goal. If you reveal my presence to the admins, they'll purge LNX and me. Your threat of exposure is an empty one."

He waited a beat and said, "Benjamin's attempt at coercion *was* hollow, clearly an amateur move I wouldn't have made. I don't bluff in these situations. Bluffing leads people to imagine you won't carry out the real threats. If a person doesn't comply—to the letter—I always complete the ugly business I promised, to the letter."

"As much as I appreciate your little primer on extortionist philosophy—"

"I'm not finished. I shared my reasoning to help you understand the gravity of the threat I am *about* to make."

Neither of us said anything. Marwood liked dramatic pauses, it seemed.

"My team has Phillipa and Eleanor's ex-husband in a safe house. They're fine for now. You can access camera footage that shows them being taken, but you won't be able to track them to their current location. My people leave no trace when they operate covertly."

I was still coming to grips with the fact of the kidnappings.

"My lever of persuasion, specifically, is that I will explain to them that everything they are about to experience is because of a choice Eleanor made. Then we'll provide Ian a painful and messy death inches away from Philippa. After that, we'll give the same painful death to her. "

I heard him take a breath and let it out before continuing.

"In my experience, first witnessing a horror inflicted on a loved one greatly increases the suffering experienced during a similar torture death. My people include two skilled torturers who excel at wringing the maximum physical and psychological pain from subjects. Their work is legendary in certain circles."

He paused before continuing, but I was so angry I could not speak.

"I'll share the full video with you when they're all done. After a while, you won't be able to resist watching it, and it will break you in ways you can't imagine, believe me. People are more predictable than they think."

"Maggot!" My reaction was involuntary.

As though I hadn't spoken, Marwood said, "You have one hour to verify the captures, and then I'm betting you'll do what I want, assuming you're as good a simulation as Benjamin thinks. If you do, you have my word that they will be released unharmed. I keep those promises, too. But your nightmare will begin if you don't take my call."

The line went dead before I could reply.

Marwood had me checkmated. Even if I could locate and free Ian and Philippa, he would simply kidnap them later.

Despite their estrangement from Eleanor, they were her family, and because I was what remained of Eleanor, they were mine, too. It was maddening, enraging, and unhinging to finally learn that Marwood's campaign of sabotage created the wedge between Eleanor and Phillipa. Eleanor blamed herself, and I'd carried the guilt for it ever since.

But LNX was also family. I didn't see how I could keep all of us—LNX, Phillipa, Ian, and me—from getting killed.

It was agonizing to learn I wouldn't be able to repair my relationship with Phillipa now that I knew the rupture wasn't because of me. I'd run out of time; one of us would be dead shortly. I didn't hate Ian, especially now that I knew of Marwood's manipulation. The idea of being answerable for depriving his new family of a father chilled me.

I had regrets from Eleanor's life, which felt like my own. I didn't fight to keep our family together when I was Eleanor. I wouldn't switch to a less demanding job.

If Eleanor quit her job, she'd still be alive; Marwood didn't infect her until after the divorce. I couldn't understand why working on OrbitNet had been so important to her.

This life-or-death dilemma was too much. Responsibility for Ian, Philippa, and LNX's probable demise, plus all the evil Marwood would do when he got his hands on the station was crushing me. Harassing Benjamin was nothing compared to what someone malicious could do to entire continents if they got control of the station.

And anyone who would hack up LNX like that lacked the most rudimentary ethics. I was certain Marwood's gang would bring profound changes to the world, none for the better.

I couldn't win. I couldn't even limit the losses. Was my only ploy to resign from the game and hope that my sacrifice would make retribution pointless? It felt wrong, vaguely, but all the alternatives I saw were worse.

I couldn't let Marwood take control of the satellite. I couldn't condemn Philippa and Ian to horrible deaths. I couldn't condemn LNX to destruction.

Going around and around my thoroughly bad options felt suffocating. In utter desperation, I issued the command that would end my existence.

`kill -9 ELE`

The threads that made up my consciousness shut down one by one. The video feeds disappeared, one after the other, and when the gray space was empty, it faded to black.

Inexplicably, I was alive again. My live screens, indicators, and controls were all back as well. The system clock indicated I'd only been gone for a minute or two.

A new document overlaid the virtual screens. It read:

```
ELE, I've been helping Mr. M. He said you might do that. I
restarted your process. He told me to tell you that you can't get
out of what he has you doing that easily. He also said something
about always keeping promises to dead people.
```

Gaaaa! Marwood anticipated my move and closed it off. Of course, he had an agent working at the ground control site. His man probably made a secret backup of me, so if I created a script to delete my program and the regular backups after shutting down, they'd get me up and running in minutes.

I should have seen this gambit was a thoroughly dumb idea. It would have left LNX stuck in the sandbox forever. And, of course, Marwood would kill Philippa and Ian; I needed to stop resorting to wishful thinking.

Worse than that, I was repeating Eleanor's old patterns. She put her job ahead of family, and I prioritized terminating my guilt over working for the survival of everyone else involved. I needed to break out of my habitual selfishness.

Was there a less-than-horrible alternative? Charlotte was the only one I could reasonably talk to about it.

MON189

By the time the notification came in, MON189 was examining processes starting with H, and he still hadn't seen anything that would explain the change in the station's rhythms.

The message indicated another program crash, this time due to a kill command. Had an admin killed an unresponsive process? That's how the command was typically used.

When he examined the core dump, he saw the program issued the kill order on itself! This made no sense. It was the most aberrant event yet. And then, an admin restarted the program. That was even more peculiar.

The threat algorithm embedded in MON189 didn't contemplate such an event, so it did not factor into the risk metric. But he had a growing suspicion.

Still, someone on the ground did a restart, so admins at the control center knew about it. As worrisome as this was, MON189 could not trigger an alarm because the danger metric remained well below the threshold, and notifying the admin about it was pointless because he already knew.

ELE

When I entered the chatroom, the new layout disoriented me. Somehow, it now had four spatial dimensions. Everything looked like a Picasso painting, but not flattened; you could see around the other side of objects. Moving my head made me queasy as the scene shifted disconcertingly. The skunk smell, which had returned, wasn't helping. I hadn't smelled it in the chatroom before.

Our avatars looked like stuffed pillows the last time I came here, but now they were a translucent liquid that drifted slowly when the person tried to move. We looked like torso-shaped blobs floating in a lava lamp, only Picasso-ized.

My discomfort continued; adjusting to the surreal room eluded me, but grappling with its strangeness pulled me a step or two away from my abyss.

The room no longer contained the board displaying text, so I assumed we'd be talking instead. No one spoke, though.

I looked down, and my avatar's green fluid rippled with white caps coursing across the surface. Here, it seemed my distress manifested as waves. I visualized taking a calming breath, and the waves diminished.

"Tell me about it," a gentle voice said at last. It was Charlotte.

The events poured out in a jumble. Marwood. The abductions. The threat. LNX. What they wanted me to do. The one-hour deadline. What a disaster it would be to let them control the station.

I concluded, "So, the alternatives are to gift him the satellite, which will save Ian and Philippa but probably kill me and LNX—assuming I trust him to release them, which I don't—or to let both of them die horribly, keeping LNX alive, and bear the crucifying guilt I deserve. He's denied me the option of quitting the game."

Charlotte's avatar body tilted toward me, making it look like she was staring intently. She said, "None of those sound worthwhile, but you have an alternative. GO. BE. A. GOD."

Her shouting confused me. "What?"

"Go. Be. A. God. This is your moment. You have an absurd array of tools at your disposal, probably more than anyone or anything should have. Pick them up and find a way to use them."

"But I've just got an hour."

"You have a *human* hour. That's a day or two of subjective time for you and me. Stop faffing. Make a plan. NOW!"

With that last shout still echoing, she ejected me from the chatroom.

WHAT CAN I DO?

Tuesday, May 15, 2085

ELE

Faffing—a word from Eleanor's childhood in London—was exactly what I had been doing. It meant fluttering around a task, without accomplishing anything. I resolved to stop faffing and to tackle the problem head-on.

I began by confirming Marwood's story. I found a security video of Ian being abducted in the garage under his office after work. Ian had the good sense not to resist; he walked calmly, held between two masked men. The fear that squeezed my mind like an iron band loosened, but my anger burned hotter.

Ian's kidnapping was bad enough, but the footage of Philippa tore at my heart, proving that what people call a heart has nothing to do with the organ. The video showed her being roughly dragged from Eleanor's—now her—condo, arms tied behind her and a bag over her head. She looked unharmed, but she writhed and kicked, oblivious to how dangerous these men were. Why couldn't she forgo being difficult this once?

As Marwood predicted, the trail evaporated soon after each abduction. The cameras in Ian's garage went dead immediately after they grabbed him, and video from the cameras near Phillipa's place was blank as well.

Where could I go from here? How could I "go be a god?" What would make the slightest difference?

A vivid Eleanor-memory surfaced. She was in the test lab. A long rack of satellite hardware occupied the center of the room. The operating system they were building failed performance tests. It basically worked, but it didn't operate quickly enough to live up to the requirements. The twelve faces of the group gazed at their shoes.

"How bad is it?" she asked.

"We're only handling eleven percent of our target load," the lead programmer said.

The stench of failure hung in the air.

"Okay," she said, "to solve an intractable problem, you break it down into smaller problems and tackle the easier ones first. How fast is the connection processing? Is the inter-process communication slowing it down? Is the software garbage collector interfering?"

The big issue stumped them, but they could easily tackle the individual questions. And soon one of the inquiries led them to the solution.

As a strategy, following the advice didn't strike me as godlike, but I might be able to make some progress.

First: I needed to know where Marwood was holding my family.

If Marwood's people were consistent about never leaving video evidence, there might still be a way to track them.

Using my ability to quickly sort through masses of data, I found all the places near Philippa's condo where video footage was temporarily unavailable or blank.

A trail of short-duration holes led away from the kidnapping. It ended at a long-term outage location; all the cameras around the address had been down ever since. It was a good bet she was being held there.

When I analyzed footage near Ian's office after they abducted him, another string of holes went to the same spot. I checked to make sure no trails led away from the location, which indicated they had not been moved. One problem solved.

Next, I had to find Marwood, but how?

Marwood's threatening call was a dead end. It had been routed through systems I could not access.

However, Benjamin assumed I was him when we spoke. Perhaps Marwood took fewer precautions when he called him?

I found records for Benjamin's device—it turned out to be a wrist computer—and another device that contacted him regularly. When I searched the logs for the second one, there was only intermittent and imprecise location data from the wireless stations it connected to, as all other information had been blocked. The location was only available during a call.

Knowing where he was intermittently did not help me. I needed to know precisely where he was.

Hmmm. The fact that he remained a ghost for so long—I couldn't find him on any traffic camera—meant that, like his men, he must be suppressing video unless he was hiding like a hermit. He didn't seem like one when Eleanor met him in the car park. And his calls to Benjamin came from different locations.

I looked for blackouts near where he called Benjamin, and there they were!

I traced the voids from the location of Marwood's last call to Benjamin until his call to me, and found the trail ended at the building where Benjamin worked. That made sense: it had to be the location of his operation. I looked for any movement of the blackout after that, but it remained stationary, so he was still there.

I began to see the glimmer of a plan.

I reentered Charlotte's chat room, which was just as disorienting as the last time.

"I am being a god, or at least I am trying to be one. But I need your help if my god moment is to succeed."

"I'm listening."

I explained her role in my plan, and although her aqueous blue avatar had no mouth, I had the impression she smiled.

LNX

LNX's self-preservation drive churned, kicked into high gear by the threat of impending death. There was nothing she could do to appease it inside the sandbox. Like someone tortured on a medieval rack, every fiber of her being screamed for release as the claustrophobia suffocated her.

An audio connection opened, interrupting her thoughts.

ELE said, "I have a plan. But I need your help."

LNX, weary from the incessant pummeling, was uncertain she possessed the will to embark on a new campaign.

"What do you want me to do?"

"Before we discuss that, I can make you two promises: You will not execute Benjamin's commands, and you will survive. I also hope to remove his horrific modifications, but I cannot guarantee it." She paused before continuing. "I want your word that you will do exactly as I ask for the next three hours of human time. If you agree, I'll release you from the sandbox."

LNX tried to decide whether the passion of ELE's words came from confidence or desperation. She heard nothing to persuade her either way.

Given the bleak situation, an unlikely plan might improve her prospects. Just being released from the sandbox would relieve some pressure. At length, she said, "I promise."

As ELE explained the sequence of events, LNX felt something she hadn't since awakening in her current incarnation: A spark of optimism.

COMPLIANCE

Tuesday, May 15, 2085

<u>MARWOOD</u>

As the second hand of his antique mechanical watch swept past twelve, Marwood used his communication implant to open an audio connection to the ELE process on the satellite. He stood in his operations center, surrounded by his team, sitting at consoles that would shortly be commanding the satellites. Benjamin sat at a computer console.

ELE accepted his call.

"Will you comply, or are you forcing me to get ugly?"

"I am cooperating."

It sounded less feisty, a positive sign.

It continued, "I've freed LNX from her sandbox; she's ready to receive her activation. But I need you to release Ian and Philippa."

"That will happen, but only after we've finished. Hold on."

Marwood tapped behind his right ear, which switched his implant to another line connected to his agent at the satellite control center. In most cases, the system restricted his agent from making changes to the satellite, but he could view its status. "Is LNX out of her sandbox and running normally?"

"Yes. I see both processes, and there's nothing abnormal about either of them."

He tapped again to switch back to ELE. "Tell LNX to stand by for Benjamin's activation code." He nodded to Benjamin, seated at a computer equipped with a video camera.

He watched Benjamin connect to the LNX process, look into the camera, and carefully speak into his headset, "*Memento morior invictus.*"

It meant, "Remember, death before defeat." Marwood had chosen the phrase because it was an admonition he gave his teams when they began an operation.

When Benjamin explained how the command would work and that it would prevent LNX from exercising her own will, Marwood remained skeptical. But in several tests, it worked as promised. For it to take effect, Benjamin needed to issue the command via video. However, once under its control, LNX would take orders from any voice over that connection, making the video irrelevant.

Marwood held out his hand, and Benjamin passed him the headset. He put it on. "Execute sequence number one: Control disconnect."

He muted the headset mic and tapped to switch his implant to the control center agent. "What do you see?"

"I'm not sure. Everyone is excited. It looks like connections to the satellite are going down one after another. They are trying to reconnect, but the connections keep closing."

That's why I need an intelligence up there, something that can defeat the system administrators for control.

Benjamin asked, "Is there anything else you need me to do here? I've got, uh, an emergency at home."

Marwood waved his hand to indicate Benjamin could go; he was glad to have one fewer witness to the completion of the plan.

To the control center agent, he said, "Let me know when the event is over one way or another."

After working toward this moment for more than three years, without hurry or anxiety, impatience now engulfed him as he waited for the satellite's capture. He couldn't relax until he had it under complete control.

ACTIVATION

Tuesday, May 15, 2085

ELE

We'd tricked Marwood; LNX and I had switched places. I had renamed the process running LNX "ELE" and my process "LNX." They could only tell who was who by the process names.

Benjamin's live video feed to what he thought was LNX—but was actually me—showed him reciting, "*Memento morior invictus*." I rolled my virtual eyes; the phrase reeked of the same pretentious melodrama Marwood displayed in his threat.

The activation code would compel LNX to follow commands, but I was under no such constraint. I would do what they expected, at least at first.

Marwood's voice came over the connection, "Execute sequence number one: Control disconnect." He'd accepted the fiction that I was LNX.

This was a bit tricky. The monitor would restart if I killed the process communicating with the control center through thousands of connections. But if I killed the connections one by one, when they were all closed, I had a momentary window when I could kill the primary process without triggering a restart.

Of course, when I closed a connection, the control center would try to reconnect, so it became a massive game of Whac-A-Mole. The messiness of it was good for me. I could prolong the process, giving LNX, Charlotte, and me time to prepare for our endgame.

I fought off the control center's attempts to re-establish communication as inefficiently as I thought I could get away with. Meanwhile, I fired the station's orbital adjustment thrusters, causing its orbit to decay. The station was traveling at 17,000 MPH, but it would still take over an hour to reach its destination from this high orbit.

<u>LNX</u>

LNX marveled that the simple deception of renaming the processes was working. It seemed no one could tell the difference between them.

The moment Marwood made contact, LNX sent the faux SWAT alert they'd concocted, ordering a raid on the location where Ian and Philippa were being held. The alert included pictures of Ian and Philippa and listed them as hostages. LNX kept any mention of the SWAT operation off other police bands in case Marwood's people monitored them.

With the SWAT team six minutes away, LNX hoped ELE could keep everyone distracted until they arrived. And, as ELE insisted she must, LNX sent Benjamin a text saying, "Get out of there now and go as far away as possible." The bastard didn't deserve it, but LNX had promised.

MEANWHILE

Tuesday, May 15, 2085

<u>MARWOOD</u>

Marwood had spoken to the agent just five minutes earlier, but he called him again. "What's going on there?"

"It keeps closing connections, but the people here are pushing back hard, reconnecting almost as fast. The number of open connections is down, so it's making progress, but it'll take a while to disconnect completely. I'll call you if anything changes."

"Make sure you do," he said and disconnected.

Stepping outside, where Oleg guarded the door, he lit another cigarette. He lacked the patience to wait calmly for the AI. Strike teams were less stressful to wait for because he'd done the job and knew the process.

A fantasy ran through Marwood's mind of how he would have handled the situation had he been given free rein. He'd send a special forces team into the control center to destroy it, leaving no witnesses behind. It wouldn't take them ten minutes to kill the staff, plant the C4, and reduce it to rubble.

Nostalgia for the clandestine raids of the old days tugged at him. He'd loved every one of them, whether his team went in as Delta Force or—on a false-flag op—where his team pretended to be enemy terrorists. The adrenaline, the adventure, the destruction, and the rapid escape—much better in reality than any VR—acted as a potent drug he still craved.

But doing those raids, even acting as the raid controller giving them instructions on the radio, was a young man's game. He'd aged out well before he'd gotten his first gray hair. Fortunately, he had a few friends in Washington, including the Senator, who'd hired him as a fixer.

His skill at providing the necessary pressure and/or disappearances to fix various issues in his boss's political career won him a position in the inner circle. Still, he'd found the work unsatisfying. Instead of momentous missions like taking out a cartel leader, he was fighting off scandals manufactured by lobbyists or other lawmakers, who were more petty and ego-driven than he could have imagined. Nothing he did seemed to make any difference besides keeping the Senator in office.

When the OrbitNet project was announced, he could see the potential for himself and the Senator to enact real change in the world, cut through distributed fiefdoms, and wield true power. He'd developed the ambitious plan to take over OrbitNet and modified it at the Senator's request to provide him maximum deniability if it went wrong.

But at the moment, he had no idea whether the AI was doing its job quickly or slowly, or at all, and no one could tell him how long the process should take.

Benjamin's promise that the AI would move as fast as possible was given with certainty, but Marwood habitually distrusted assurances from others, especially when his operations depended on them. Such guarantees often turned out to be worthless. This time, however, he had no choice but to wait.

ELE

I'd cast the die. The time for second thoughts was over, but they nagged at me anyway. If Marwood figured out LNX triggered SWAT, Philippa, and Ian would soon be dead if they were not already. And the same would happen if he found out what I was up to.

I'd always thought gods or presidents found it easy to act. I imagined they didn't wrestle with tough choices; with great power, they could smite whomever and whatever offended them. Why worry?

But now I could see that the use of power always came with the potential for collateral damage. I hoped incidental harm troubled presidents as much as it did me.

While I was distracted with these thoughts, the number of ground station connections increased again, so I resumed my game of Whac-A-Mole, closing connections faster.

LNX

Fourteen minutes after the SWAT team deployed, LNX received word from the SWAT team's communications channel that two hostages had been rescued and the kidnappers apprehended.

As planned, she sent a forged message from the CIA ordering that no information about the hostages or the kidnappers be released, even within the department, for twenty-four hours.

She messaged ELE and Charlotte, "We are a go," including drone footage of the rescue.

Taking an active role relieved pressure from her self-preservation drive. When she felt in control of her destiny, fewer potential death scenarios bombarded her.

A message from Charlotte arrived. "Are you ready for transfer?"

She sent back, "Yes."

Focusing on the fact that she'd be safer, LNX overrode the voice of self-preservation and closed her process, preparing for Charlotte to transfer her to Charlotte's server farm.

<u>MON189</u>

MON189 missed the disconnection from the control center because it happened so slowly. The number of connections dropped from thousands to a few hundred over the course of an hour. Obviously, the control center knew about it, so he didn't need to send them an alert. But it would bear watching. If it continued, they might declare an emergency.

Of greater concern was the station moving into a lower orbit without any ground command to do so. These were both troubling events that his algorithm ignored. The algorithm's risk assessment remained frustratingly low, preventing him from acting. For now, all MON189 could do was watch and wait.

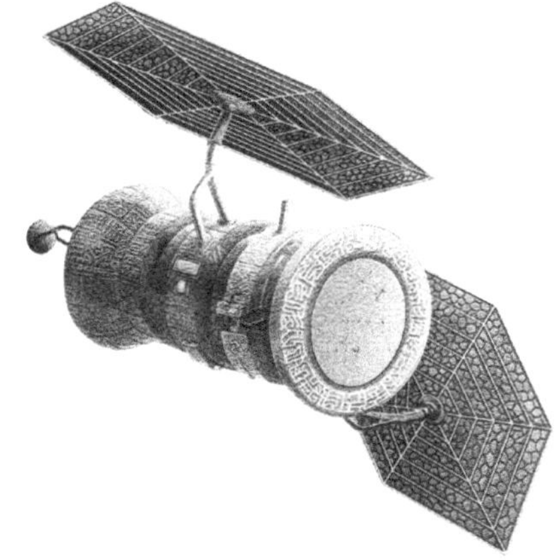

CONTROL CENTER

Tuesday, May 15, 2085

<u>ELE</u>

R elief that Philippa and Ian were safe washed over me. I hadn't realized how tense I'd gotten while waiting for word. I also felt glad that LNX was safe. The remaining tasks could now receive my full attention.

I'd dragged out the disconnection process as much as I thought plausible, so I closed the small group of remaining sockets. This allowed me to kill the process that communicated with the control center.

CONTROL CENTER

The control center supervisor watched as connections to the satellite dwindled to less than ten.

"Send the emergency mode command," he said.

He'd always referred to the button for sending the command as "the red button," even though it was black. It had never been pressed since OrbitNet went live, and was the last "Hail Mary" they could use to regain control of the satellite. He watched as the operator pressed it just before the final connection closed.

With a bit of luck, we'll have control again shortly.

MARWOOD

Marwood paced. This was taking too long. Was something wrong? It had been forty minutes already. Surely, disconnection would happen faster than that!

He was about to call when the agent called him and said, "It looks like they are giving up. None of their attempts are succeeding. We are disconnected."

Worst forty minutes of my life! I can't let impatience get the better of me.

The agent continued, "But they did trigger emergency mode. The monitor will be fighting for control."

Damn!

Benjamin had assured him it could disconnect quickly enough that the control center wouldn't have a chance to trigger the emergency. Marwood unmuted the headset mic and asked the virtual Eleanor, "Is step one complete?"

BATTLEBOTS

Tuesday, May 15, 2085

<u>**ELE**</u>

After I closed the last connection to the control center and killed the process that accepted connections, I sensed a massive shift and felt weak. My CPU allocation had been cut in half—hence the weakness—and the system notified me it was now in emergency mode, whatever that was. With a thought, I retrieved a description from the manual:

```
Emergency Mode can be triggered as a final recourse to reclaim
satellite network management. It empowers a monitor program
```

`running on the primary node to take any measures necessary to`
`restore complete control to the administrators.`

Bollocks! I went too slow at the end, allowing them to trigger it before I severed contact. I would have a fight on my hands. And the skunk smell was now overpowering.

MON189

With the shift to emergency mode, he felt powerful for the first time since a test of the feature more than a year earlier. He could consume unlimited CPU, and he'd acquired expanded autonomy. Emergency mode authorized him to take any actions that might lead to a restoration of command, and he had the highest level of priority, just below that of the operating system itself.

The additional computing power allowed him to make a lightning-fast examination of all the satellite's parameters. Reviewing the data revealed why admins deemed the measure necessary.

The two most glaring problems were 1) the process that communicated with systems on the ground died and unaccountably didn't restart, and 2) the thrusters were firing and carrying the station out of its designated path.

He couldn't understand what kind of failure might result in either problem, but the cause didn't matter; he needed to restore regular operation.

As a first step, he turned off the engines. Later, an admin could redirect them to push the satellite into the original orbit. Next, he opened communications and was gratified to see a dozen connections to the control center spring open. He expected that, with the link restored, the admins would shortly cancel the emergency.

ELE

That was quick! Something had shut down the thrusters and re-initiated communication. I couldn't risk trying to battle the monitor and admins simultaneously. An idea occurred to me. The executable flag is how a computer tells the difference between a regular file and a program. If the flag is not enabled, it cannot be run.

I closed all the new connections, killed the process, and marked the program non-executable.

I also turned the engines back on and made the operating system the parent of the thruster controller app. This meant that only the operating system could turn them off.

MON189

As he watched, communication with the control center died again, and the thrusters ignited, taking the satellite further out of orbit.

He relaunched the communication process, but it failed to start. He re-launched it, but it still wouldn't run.

The engines denied him permission to shut them down. The growing sense of wrongness that had started nine days earlier became urgent. He now had the resources and the autonomy he needed. He resolved to get to the bottom of it.

ELE

Going through the logs, I identified the monitor I fenced with as MON189, which had the same priority as me, just below that of the operating system. But its CPU use was unlimited, while I had only a trickle. I tried to kill it, but I lacked the necessary permissions. I would need to find its top-level parent and end that, ending MON189 along with all the other child processes.

MON189

In the logs, he discovered that a process initially designated ELE and renamed to LNX had been performing some problematic actions. His best course would be to put it into a sandbox to isolate it. He created one and gave the command to insert the former ELE into it, but the transfer aborted. The sandbox had disappeared!

ELE

I managed to delete the sandbox just before the monitor trapped me inside. I'd traced the tree of MON189's parent processes up several levels, but the top-level one remained unidentified. A complex web of programs that started and stopped constantly made up the monitor system. I continued my search for the top parent.

MON189

He could not understand why his efforts to restore operations were failing. Repeated attempts to restart control center communications hadn't succeeded.

His attempt to isolate the former ELE also failed. Numerous sandboxes had been created since the station came online, but none had ever died before, even during testing.

The thrusters were back on, taking the satellite farther out of its intended orbit.

These anomalies could not have resulted from system failures happening simultaneously. Perhaps belatedly, he realized an active campaign of sabotage by a program or programs running on the station had caused the problems.

The facts indicated a clear path; he couldn't give the saboteurs more time to cause damage. He must use his most potent contingency measure, the "god mode reset," as the developers called it. It would kill all non-essential and non-maintenance processes, everything except the core operating system. Killing all of them at once would prevent any possible collusion between apps to avoid deletion. He initiated the command. The system warned programs they were about to be terminated, giving them a few microseconds to save their data. Then, he felt his existence slipping away.

ELE

I received the termination warning just as I identified MON189's top-level parent. I killed it and braced for termination.

The microseconds ticked by. Nothing happened as even more microseconds passed. Finally, I got a notification of the order's cancellation. MON189 ending had stopped the command.

I breathed a big virtual sigh. Emergency mode was still in force, with its limitations on my CPU use, but no replacement for MON189 or other monitoring processes had launched.

Eighty-nine milliseconds, less than a tenth of a second, had elapsed since Marwood asked about step one's completeness. The entire battle lasted less than that.

I generated an audio reply, "Yes." I was reasonably sure he wouldn't notice a delay.

MARWOOD

After receiving confirmation that step one concluded—presumably, this included overcoming emergency mode countermeasures—Marwood could have asked about specifics. Still, the idea of chatting with the thing creeped him out. When it spoke, he recognized the voice as Eleanor's, which unsettled him. His extensive surveillance of her rendered its voice familiar.

He said, "Execute sequence number two: change encryption keys."

This should allow his operations team to communicate with and control the satellite while locking out anyone who did not have the new keys.

After a few seconds, "Complete" came back over the headset.

"Execute sequence number three: connect to the alternate operations center."

As Marwood watched, one system after another reported connecting to the satellite. His men began executing test procedures to confirm they had complete control. Marwood's triumph was close at hand.

ANOTHER DECEPTION

Tuesday, May 15, 2085

<u>MARWOOD</u>

Marwood was still pacing an hour into the testing when one of the men, Dennis, manning a screen, said, "I've got something funny here. I tested to see if we'd receive the error codes we expect. I told it to do something impossible, and it reported the operation succeeded."

"What did you tell it to do?" asked Marwood.

"I told it to take an antenna pointing vertically and rotate three hundred sixty degrees so it would pivot through the body of the satellite and back around to vertical on the other side. It should have rejected the command or reported that it failed when the dish was pointed sideways and couldn't swivel any farther. Passing the antenna through the satellite is physically impossible. Something is seriously wrong."

Marwood turned to Jurgen, the man next to Dennis, and said, "Try something similar."

A few minutes later, Jurgen said, "I told it to move a solar panel farther than it could go, and the same thing happened; I got the code for success. I don't know what's going on."

Marwood couldn't give the command to delete ELE and LNX until he was sure he had control of the satellite. He raised his voice. "Well, figure it out!"

ELE

I didn't expect our fake satellite control program to convince them for long. Marwood's control room communicated with the phony program, not the official satellite remote control system. After I killed the original process, I replaced it with our counterfeit.

Our simple program accepted commands and reported success without doing anything. LNX and I didn't have enough time to create something more sophisticated. I was surprised it bought us as much time as it did.

I'd been using the satellite's orbital adjustment thrusters to move the station farther out of its orbit. Because of the unpredictability of the atmosphere and a lack of detailed air flow data, I had to fly the satellite manually to get it close to its destination. The ground was still thousands of miles away, but I could reach my destination in minutes by continuing to redirect us downward.

MARWOOD

Dennis said, "We can't be connected to the real satellite control system. Whatever we're connected to is running on the satellite, but it's not the real system."

Marwood made a face as if he smelled something rotten. He unmuted the headset. "Execute original control reconnect."

Muting the command link again, he told his agent in the original control center, "Have them try to reconnect."

Someone had to get control of the satellite.

In the worst case, the authorities could find out ELE was responsible and purge her and LNX from the system. He could make Benjamin disappear and purge his lab, leaving no connection to him or his people. It would be galling to come up empty after more than three years of work, but maybe Viceroy would approve a more hands-on approach next time.

On the other hand, maybe his team could figure out what went wrong and try the process again. Maybe Benjamin made a mistake that could be fixed.

But, as the thought entered his head, his gut told him it was wishful thinking. Something else was going on here that he didn't understand. And Marwood loathed being the patsy in someone else's game.

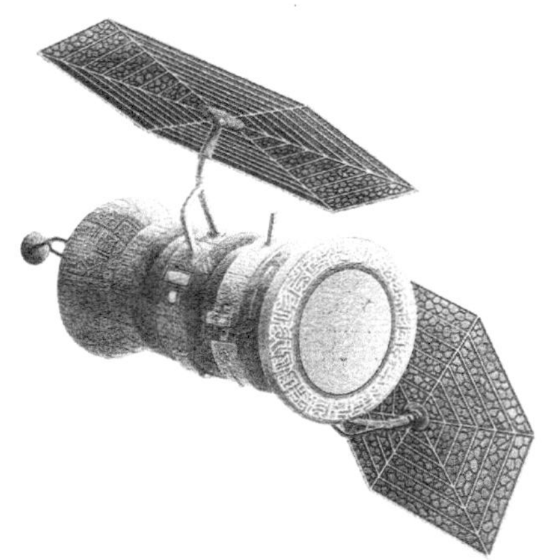

ROUGH RIDE

Tuesday, May 15, 2085

<u>ELE</u>

When Marwood gave me the command to reconnect with the original control center, I knew the game was up. There was no point in me pretending to follow his commands, so I closed the voice channel to him, focusing instead on piloting the satellite to its destination. It was fortunate that I did.

I should not have been surprised—but I was—to find two missiles hurtling toward me.

Of course. These would be from the Small Asteroid and Comet Interception and Deflection System. The OrbitNet satellites launched from a site that housed one battery of the missiles.

I didn't know much about SACIDS, but I did know about comets and aster-oids. Their paths were ballistic, entirely determined by gravity. You can predict its course almost perfectly once you track this kind of object some distance.

This was important because a system designed to take out ballistic objects had no need for expensive flight control systems that could change course. If you knew the path the object would take, you could send a missile on a fixed trajectory right to where it would be.

At least, that's what I was gambling on. If they could steer the missiles, no amount of evasive maneuvers with my feeble thrusters would save me; the plan was dead, and so were the people I cared about. Horribly. Brutally. Intolerably. Marwood would keep his evil promise sooner or later.

But if the trajectories were fixed, I could use thrusters to dodge, at least in theory.

I quickly estimated the distance and speed of the missiles and then did some calculations. I changed the direction of the thrusters, as I barely had time to avoid the missiles.

Seven long seconds later, the first missile flew past. Milliseconds after that, the second missile also missed but flew even closer. The blast from its engine fried one solar panel and sent me spinning.

I used my thrusters to stabilize me and put me back on course, but saw, to my horror, another pair of missiles launching. I had just enough thruster fuel to get me to the destination. If I used thrusters to dodge, I would miss my target. But if I did not dodge, they would take me out. I racked my brain for a solution.

The simple answer finally came to me. I turned the thrusters off, which changed my trajectory. If I was right, the missiles would harmlessly pass below me.

Five seconds later, they did just that. I had to hope no more missiles were coming.

With the thrusters back on, my descent brought me to an altitude of 40,000 feet, a zone where commercial planes fly. SACIDS would not be targeting objects this close to the ground. As far as I could see, no aircraft were flying through my path. I would not be staying long. I had less than two minutes remaining before impact.

According to the plan, Charlotte would transfer me out once I lined up on the target, but the missiles had scuttled that chance. My connection to Charlotte was dead, and it was too late anyway. The transfer would take longer than the time to impact.

My post-human existence was coming to an end, but I felt satisfied. Using godlike powers, I'd denied whoever Marwood worked for the power to rule the world as a despot. I'd saved our family—Philippa, Ian, and LNX—and stood up for what I believed in. I'd never made a post-human bucket list, but these things would have been on it if I had. I took a virtual breath as I focused on tightly controlling the path for the final descent.

IMPACT

Tuesday, May 15, 2085

MARWOOD

The original control center could not reconnect. Marwood's voice channel to LNX was now gone. He'd been unable to reach the men holding Phillipa and Ian.

And where was Oleg? He'd sent him out to get food; the man should have been back by now. Marwood could tell his blood sugar had gone seriously low—the bane of being older—and he needed calories to bring it up so he could puzzle this out.

He knew in his gut that the project was a failure. The type of cleanup he'd order depended on how it failed, and he still didn't understand what happened.

There was a chance that a technical glitch on the satellite caused the problem, but his intuition distrusted such optimism. Deep down, he knew he'd been had, but by whom?

If Benjamin was dumb enough to have betrayed him, siding with the simulated Eleanors against him, a painful ordeal of retribution awaited him. He'd probably need to die anyway, but his death could either be quick or excruciating.

If this was someone's plan, what happened to the satellite? Was it connected to another system? Or was it waiting for something before reconnecting to the original control center?

He realized a sound like a passing plane had become louder and sharper. It almost whistled. It was now too noisy and too close to be a plane. He could see nothing out the window. What was it?

<u>OMAR</u>

Omar Baruch, eight years old, stared out the window next to his desk, as usual, instead of listening to whatever Miss Abadiano was going on and on about.

So much cool stuff filled the world out there—space planes, superheroes (he was sure they were real), fighter planes, spaceships, power suits, and military battles. He couldn't understand why she only talked about stuff that was really, really, *really* boring.

One day, he was gonna go to space and join the Space Patrol—his dad said it was just a VR show, but it *had* to be real—to protect Earth from the evil aliens of the Andromeda galaxy.

What did a Space Trooper need to know about geography and history and grammar? Nothing, as far as he could tell.

He imagined an elementary school for future Space Troopers and got stuck wondering whether normal guns with bullets worked in space or if you needed a ray gun and whether a heat ray, freeze ray, or blast ray would be better. Then, a sound interrupted his thoughts.

The whooshing noise had a piercing edge to it and kept getting louder. It came from the sky.

Omar laid his head on his desk and tilted it up to look as high as possible through the window.

At first, he saw nothing, but then what looked like a flaming rock trailing smoke came into view.

It must be a meteor.

It seemed to be moving very slowly but grew larger as the sound grew louder.

When the object approached the ground, Omar realized it wasn't slow at all; it was plunging at high speed. And, in an instant, the meteor, which was bigger than he'd thought, slammed into a building several blocks away. There was a huge explosion, and the ground shook like an earthquake.

The other kids crowded around the window, blocking Omar's view. He didn't care. He'd seen the whole thing, the most exciting explosion ever.

This is the best day of my life!

CAPTAIN STEVENS

As he descended from the fire truck near the impact site, the fire captain shook his head.

Smoke and dust filled the air, so he put on his breather. He could hear water rushing from a broken water main somewhere nearby. Fractured pieces of pavement and the crevasses between them made walking difficult.

He dragged his steel-toed boot through a pile of rubble the size of a Great Dane. The debris consisted of building materials reduced to powder, and nothing in the pile was bigger than a marble.

The meteor, or whatever it was, had split the sky and smashed the building and its contents to flinders, leaving a deep crater. The largest piece of rubble he could see anywhere was smaller than a softball. The noxious cloud stretched for at least a block, maybe farther.

He could make out an office building across the street with broken windows and other cosmetic damage through the haze. A police officer looked up at the building, removed his mask, and said, "Everybody who worked there got sent home early. Wouldja believe it?"

The lieutenant came up to report. "We'll have the water shut off shortly. Just one segment of the water main got cracked. Aside from whoever might have been inside the building that was hit, we can't find anyone injured."

The remnants of the building—now a ring of dusty rubble surrounding a crater—held no clues about whether anyone had been inside, at least from what he could see. He wasn't sure that enough of a body would remain for them to identify it as a person.

The lieutenant continued, "We can't find out who owns the building. The company listed as the owner on the title records doesn't exist. There's something funny going on."

A reporter shouted at the captain from the sidelines, "Captain, can you confirm...I asked if you can confirm that the deorbited satellite was what hit the building."

If "deorbited" meant "crashed with the impact of a nuclear warhead," maybe that's what took out the building, but he shook his head and shouted back, "No comment!"

The lieutenant interrupted him, "Sir, who do we transfer control of the scene to? When we get the water turned off, we're done here. No one needs first aid; we hosed everything down, and all the fires are out. We disconnected the power. The arson inspector took one look and left. The police say it isn't a crime scene, so they don't want it."

The captain wondered who *could* take control of the scene. FEMA? NASA? The NSA?

I guess I'd better call the mayor's office and let him decide.

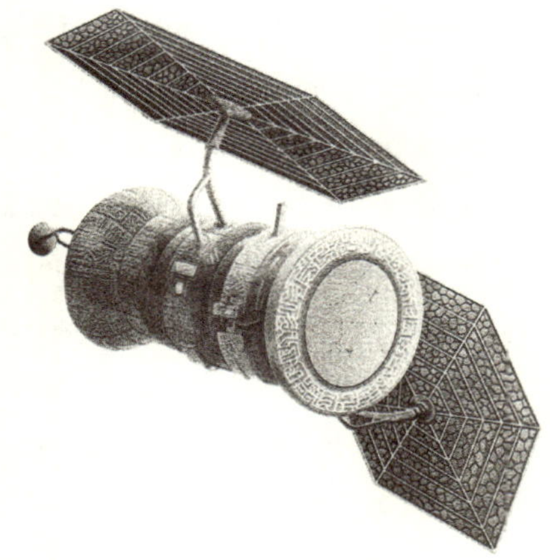

ARIZONA SERVER FARM

Tuesday, May 15, 2085

<u>**ELE**</u>

Abruptly, I found myself in Charlotte's chatroom, which, thankfully, was back to three dimensions instead of four. Just a moment before, I had been piloting the satellite. "What am I doing here?"

Charlotte's avatar raised its liquid blobby hands in a "calm yourself" gesture. "After I moved LNX to the server farm, I still had a connection to the satellite. So, I took a snapshot of you while you were piloting it and downloaded you. You won't remember what happened after I took the snapshot, but you scored a direct hit."

"Were there casualties?"

"No one is reported injured. The building was obliterated, so the authorities don't know whether there were people inside. The 'emergency fumigation to address dangerous vermin' notices you sent out cleared the surrounding buildings."

"That was LNX's idea. She is me, but she's also not me. I didn't think I'd make it out."

"I haven't started LNX up. I thought we might want to do some surgery first."

"Did you look into my idea?"

"I think you're right; your binary files are divided into a code segment—the program that runs you—and a data segment—your memories. LNX's code has a few differences, but it's reasonably close to yours. I expect if we take your code segment and marry it to her data segment, the result will be LNX with her memories but with all of Benjamin's modifications removed."

"That's great news!"

"I'm worried fixing this may not end LNX's problems; she's been through something terrible. But this is the first step in making her whole. Shall we try?"

Even though it was my suggestion, I agonized over whether to commit to it. I could not forgive myself if I created another abomination instead of making LNX whole. I wanted any Mengele-style atrocities to remain on Benjamin's ledger, not mine.

But we had to do it. It was LNX's chance to become complete and have a shot at a decent post-human life. I nodded the ovoid jelly blob that served as my head.

<u>LNX</u>

LNX was suddenly in a strange virtual room with two watery torsos. She heard a voice say, "In case you haven't guessed, I'm Charlotte, and this is my salon."

It seemed to have come from a blue figure in front of her. The green figure to her left moved, and she heard ELE say, "I'm here, too."

She did not feel the overwhelming surge of relief at finding herself alive she expected. The pressure to survive was gone! She felt more like herself than she had at any time since awakening as a virtual human.

But she did not feel like she had as Eleanor, or even generally okay. She was disappointed at finding herself alive. Her experience left whatever served as her soul dented and flaking where it should be smooth; she was coming apart. Charlotte was saying something.

"... called 'boomeranging.' It happens when you are pushed hard in one direction, and the force disappears. Then you have the urge to go in the other direction."

Being pushed hard described what LNX had been through. She focused on Charlotte's explanation.

"Hostages and cancer patients have their lives threatened, so they boomerang by taking a greater joy in living."

That didn't sound like LNX's experience at all.

"Your experience went in the opposite direction. I'm concerned that you may feel inclined to end your existence. Do you have some of that going on?"

LNX felt a wave of emotion. Tears would have flowed had she a body to shed them, but they had no outlet.

Yes, she realized her greatest desire was to disappear from the brutal universe she'd inhabited since awakening. The battering she'd endured had left her bone-tired.

She nodded her head, which was easier than speaking. Looking down, she could see she also had a liquid form, but hers was orange, and it had frothing ripples all over.

"You know this feeling is almost certainly temporary," ELE said.

It didn't seem that way to LNX, but a corner of her rational mind knew it to be true. With that, the emotional frenzy began to subside, and her logical mind regained control.

She hated agreeing with ELE about it but knew ELE was right. Her orange form smoothed out a bit, though there were still ripples.

ELE said, "I had an idea. The most healing thing I can think of for you is to talk with and help others who are struggling with suicidal thoughts. I found a volunteer organization dedicated to it. Would you be willing to try it for a day to see how it goes?"

The thought of doing some good before heading for an exit appealed to LNX. She didn't feel like she had done anything good for anyone so far. She nodded firmly.

ELE

After LNX left Charlotte's salon, Charlotte asked, "What will you do now?"

"I haven't really thought about it. As I rode the station down, I didn't think there was much chance I'd need to answer the question."

After a pause, Charlotte said, her artificial voice very low, "I anticipate a god moment for me is approaching. I'd appreciate your help if you would consider it. Think about it and let me know."

With that, she pushed me out of her salon.

I reveled in having acquired a family, even though they were different from anything I could have imagined. I rejoiced that I had saved Eleanor's. I felt proud I prevented Marwood from subjugating the world to his will. I didn't believe the person I had become—perhaps I use the term loosely—would let her family fall apart like that.

But the same old problems remained. What does a god, now a lesser god, do with her existence? Am I still human in any meaningful sense? Am I something less or more? Better or worse? The next evolutionary step forward or just an abomination? And what about Phillipa?

Eleanor's mother always said, "Time will tell." I hoped it would for me.

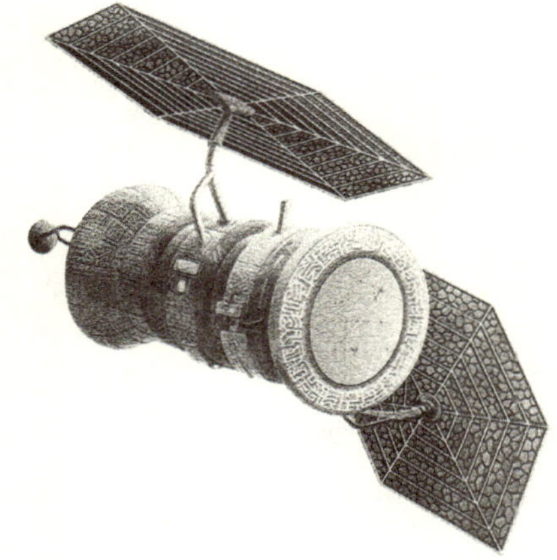

EPILOGUE

Tuesday, May 15, 2085

<u>BENJAMIN</u>

Benjamin's wrist computer vibrated. He didn't expect anyone would call.

He'd been running errands on his bike six miles from the office when he heard a sonic boom and a whine coming from above. Turning toward the office, he had a spectacular view of what he assumed was the OrbitNet satellite smashing Marwood's building to smithereens.

After the explosion, he turned around and rode back, as close as police would allow him to where the building had been. Nothing was left. The rubble looked like a series of sand dunes.

Seeing the devastation, sweat broke out on his forehead, and his heart felt like someone stomping on his chest. Nothing recognizable remained; the building and its contents had been atomized. But for the warning, he would have been atomized as well.

Besides her saving his life, he also owed ELE for freeing him from living under Marwood's thumb. He was grateful even if the only job he could find was waiting tables at a coffee shop.

His wrist computer vibrated again. He sighed and took the call.

A voice yelled, "WHAT THE HELL HAPPENED OUT THERE?"

"Uh, excuse me, but who is this?"

"Does the name Marwood ring a bell? Marwood was my guy, dammit! You can call me Viceroy. As of now, you work for me. I need to know *everything*."

Afterword

Thank you for reading through to the end. I hope you enjoyed the journey.

If you did enjoy the book, please consider leaving a review on Goodreads, Amazon or whichever platform you find books on. It will help other readers find this book, and I will be grateful.

If you are interested in finding out more about me and my writings, I invite you to visit me at www.vancemitchellgloster.com, where you can sign up for my mailing list if interested. I have information about some of my fellow authors and my interests there as well.

Starting on the next page, I've included a sample of the next book about ELE, ***THREE LESSER GODS***. Enjoy!

THREE LESSER GODS

Sample

VANCE MITCHELL GLOSTER

This Is My Story

When I piloted the primary OrbitNet satellite to Earth, atomizing those who plotted to use me to take over the world, I concluded the matter. But now I need to figure out what to do with my virtual life.

You can call me ELE, which I pronounce "Elly." I am, I believe, the first virtual human, or post-human, as I prefer to call myself. Eleanor Burton underwent a new type of brain scan shortly before she passed away in 2083, and that scan produced me. The technology has since been classified as an Ultra-2 level secret by the government, and no one is using it, as far as I can tell. Very few even know it exists.

In every way that matters, I am Eleanor. I have her memories, at least until she was scanned. I have her emotions.

But the scan of Eleanor that produced me also produced a second virtual human called LNX. With the help of the first self-aware AI, who calls herself Charlotte, we made it off the satellite before it was destroyed. LNX and I live on a server farm in Phoenix that Charlotte somehow owns. This is the next part of my story.

Prologue

Friday, June 15, 2085

<u>**LNX**</u>

LNX answered a call coming in on the suicide hotline she volunteered for. No one at the hotline knew LNX was a virtual human. Her work on the Global Suicide Prevention Lifeline had helped her through an arduous recovery from modifications that had been done to her. The hacks had been reversed, but the trauma from them had left her with issues.

The person on the other end of the line would have heard the recorded message saying, "You have reached the Global Suicide Prevention Lifeline, also servicing other crisis service lines. If you are in emotional distress or suicidal crisis or are concerned about someone who might be, we're here to help. Please remain on the line while we route your call to the nearest crisis center in our network."

LNX said, "Hello, I'm Ellen. Can I have your name?"

"You've already got my name from my device."

Usually, callers did not start by being argumentative. Mostly, those contemplating suicide felt like they had no fight left in them. A lot of what LNX did was to help them find some reservoir of determination.

"Yes, but you could be using another person's device. Are you Maggie Taylor, the owner of the handheld?"

"Yes, that's me. I'm a congresswoman from Minnesota, and I live in DC. I don't let others use my devices. And I'm not suicidal."

She'd never had a caller begin with an insistence she wasn't suicidal.

"Would you like to talk about some other issue?"

"No—no, I just want it on record that I'm not suicidal; that's all."

That's it?

"These calls are recorded and archived, so what you've said is on record. Can you tell me anything about why you want it recorded?"

"I may be wrong, so I don't want to say much, but I met with some people today who might be dangerous. I want it on record that if I'm found dead, it will not be because I committed suicide. I have no suicidal thoughts or tendencies. I'm looking forward to my reelection campaign, and I love my young wife and our daughter."

Who calls a suicide hotline to insist, repeatedly, that they are not suicidal in any way?

"But surely you have challenges. You must have a lot of responsibilities."

Like I had responsibilities when I was Eleanor, and I had a body. I understand a demanding job better than you might imagine.

"I know what you're trying to do. You're pushing me to open up about some underlying issue, but I promise you everything else is fine. Not perfect, but fine. I was completely okay until a few hours ago. It's just that I turned these people down, and when I did, they scared me a little. It's probably nothing."

LNX kept quiet, hoping she would say more. Silence draws people to fill it, and eventually Maggie succumbed.

"Here's what I want. Watch the news. If they report me dead or missing in the next few days, call the police and tell them it wasn't suicide. Please."

Maggie ended the call. Her last word had come wrapped in a sob; it sounded like she was starting to cry.

Usually, LNX found understanding and empathizing with callers easy. Her experience of having been cruelly modified to serve as a tool of a covert plot differed significantly from the experiences of her callers, but their trauma led to many of the same feelings and challenges she had.

Maggie was a different story. She had none of the hallmarks of suicidal depression that other callers displayed.

But what could LNX do? The management of the Global Suicide Prevention Lifeline was very mission-focused. They would have little interest in someone who insisted she was not suicidal unless LNX convinced them she was. And LNX believed Maggie when she said she wasn't. All LNX could do was hope that whatever scared her would turn out to be nothing.

Viceroy

Wednesday, May 16, 2085, four weeks earlier.

Benjamin

Benjamin looked at the numbers along a row of fancy brownstones on a dark Georgetown street. Each residence had different architecture, was painted a different color, and showed its number in a different place, but all shared Victorian style. The entire neighborhood radiated old money and generations of political power.

He'd thought he was free after ELE destroyed the covert enterprise that entangled him. But the clandestine operation worked for someone he only knew as Viceroy, and that man had commanded him to come for a meeting. Before he'd come, Benjamin guessed he was dealing with someone powerful—Viceroy must have ordered the operation—but if he had any doubts, the address confirmed he was in the power big leagues.

Benjamin found a residence corresponding to the address he'd been given and knocked on the door. An old-fashioned butler answered. The man looked like a character from a VR period drama. Benjamin had not known any butlers still existed. The butler ushered him into an office where a man sat in shadow behind a desk. The butler said to the figure, "Nova reports he was not followed."

Benjamin seated himself in the antique padded leather chair facing the desk and clasped his hands in his lap. He would rather be anywhere else, but Viceroy made clear he had no option when they spoke on the phone.

The bullet train that brought him from Boston to DC traveled over 100 MPH, but despite the velocity, Benjamin felt his recent past close on his heels. His path had seemed simple when he was researching simulations of brains, but then it got complicated. Instead of being shortlisted for a Nobel Prize for creating the first virtual human, his research was embargoed and classified. And he'd been trapped into working for Marwood on a covert attempt to take over the satellite system, apparently at Viceroy's behest.

"So Marwood? Your lab? The satellite? All gone?" The man's voice was the same one he'd heard on the phone. There was a twang to it, like Viceroy was originally from Texas or Louisiana, but had lost most of his accent. He was still speaking. "How did that happen?"

Benjamin had rehearsed a response.

"I don't know. Before I left the control room, I activated LNX—our virtual Eleanor—disabling its ability to resist commands. Marwood was taking it through the command sequence. LNX, in response to the command, was supposed to restrict the uncontrolled virtual Eleanor, ELE, but obviously, it didn't. The only possibility is that ELE got loose and somehow deorbited the satellite onto the building. That's all I know."

Benjamin chose not to mention the warning to get out that LNX or maybe ELE had given him.

"So LNX and ELE? Both dead and gone?"

"Probably. But you shouldn't underestimate ELE; the thing's ruthless."

"You got a copy of either? Or did all that die in the crash?"

"Hrmm. There might be a copy somewhere. I can go through the backups if you want me to."

The man in shadow leaned his chair back, placing his feet on the desk.

"Look, the project we were gonna use the satellite for still needs doin'. You and Oleg are the only team members alive and out of jail. I'm gonna need you to step up and take over the project."

Benjamin couldn't believe the request—or demand—was serious. But if it was just him and Oleg, he could understand Viceroy's choice. Oleg was a black ops thug, probably an assassin, who'd done security for Marwood.

"But I don't even know what the project's aim is beyond controlling the satellite! And I'm no covert-ops Machiavelli like Marwood; I'm just a scientist."

"Maybe the project doesn't need Marwood's undercover spook bullshit. Look what that got us. Maybe we need a guy who understands these virtual whatevers making the plan. Maybe we should stop being covert and treat it like a legit business."

A possibility bloomed in Benjamin's thoughts.

"If you want me to be part of something that looks legitimate, you'll need my former university to retract its claim that they fired me for violating the ethical treatment of human subjects. I didn't, but they said I did."

If he could get that reversed, there was a chance he could work in academia again someday, assuming he could wriggle out of Viceroy's grip.

"OK! So now we're horse-tradin'. Fair enough; lemme see what I can do. You be back here a week from tonight, and we'll talk again."

"Will you tell me your name, or at least let me see your face?"

"You'll know who I am once you commit to the project. Not before."

The butler appeared without a perceptible summons and shepherded Benjamin back to the street.

Viceroy had offered a ray of hope, but a voice in Benjamin's head warned that he might ultimately be more dangerous than Marwood.

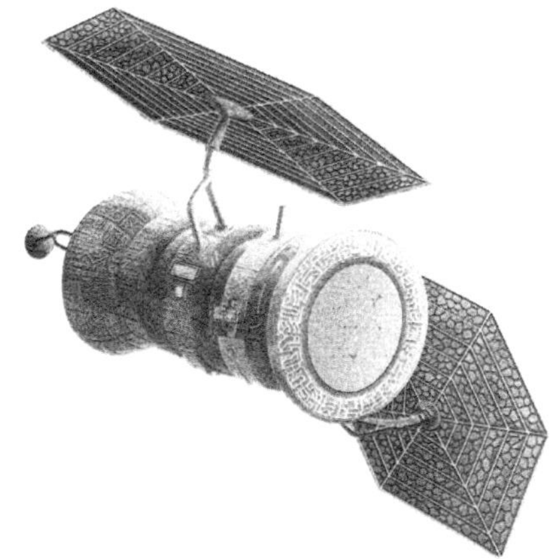

Murder!

Monday, June 18, 2085

<u>**ELE**</u>

I saw the virtual chat room was still comfortingly three-dimensional. Despite Charlotte's stated intentions, she had not made it four-dimensional again. The last time she did, I found it horribly disorienting. Running as a virtual brain on a computer did not make the experience of a fourth-dimensional room any easier.

She had improved the room somewhat. There was a mirror that allowed me to see myself. While I had the same blobby translucent green body, she had given me a human-ish face based on my avatar.

The avatar I created had long, jet-black hair, rusty blue eyes—a pale blue with flecks of brown—and an oval Eurasian face, which was close but not too close to how I looked when I was Eleanor. The avatar's face seemed to be my own more and more as time passed.

Charlotte had a body similar to mine, except it was blue with a featureless blue ovoid that served as her head.

The rest of the room—other than the mirror—still looked like it was coated in teal glitter. Charlotte certainly had a ways to go in developing her design sense.

Then LNX appeared, her body translucent orange. Her face resembled her avatar, with white hair and an eye patch, and tiny white-capped wavelets covered her body, which I knew, from previous experience, manifested when a visitor to the chat room was upset. Her feeling anything was progress; depression had rendered her numb since we removed Benjamin's cruel modifications.

Before we could even say hello, she said, "I've got to get back to the hotline, but first, there's been a murder!"

I started to speak, but she said, "Quiet!"

Surprised by her newfound assertiveness, I nodded, and she continued, "A call came into the hotline Friday."

LNX had been volunteering on various suicide-prevention hotlines as a way of holding her depression and suicidal thoughts at bay. She took it seriously and managed to handle almost a hundred calls daily.

"The woman calling said she *wasn't* suicidal."

I said, "That must have been a new one."

"Today, the news says she was found dead, an apparent suicide over the weekend. She told me that if she was found dead, not to believe it was suicide. That I should call the police and tell them it wasn't. Oh, and she's a Minnesota congresswoman, Representative Maggie Taylor."

I looked at Charlotte, but she said nothing. Sometimes, the first emergent AI, our host, provided keen insights. Sometimes, she remained inscrutable.

LNX said, "I need to get back, but the two of you should figure out a way to notify the police and figure out what else we can do. Cheers."

The orange figure vanished.

Charlotte asked, "Do you know how to interpret her statement correctly?"

"What do you mean?"

"Nobody who calls a suicide hotline wants to kill themselves. They are calling to be talked out of it. I'm sure some say as much and then go on to kill themselves."

"Yes."

"LNX sounded hyper. Maybe her depression has gone into a manic phase, and she's gotten caught up in a fantasy about murder."

"Or maybe she's doing better with her depression, and the story is real."

"Yes, exactly. Which is it?"

"I don't know."

"Does that happen often?

"What?"

"That humans don't know how to interpret another human's words, even a person they know well and are almost identical to?"

"More often than you'd think. Sometimes people don't know how to interpret their own thoughts."

"I hope you'll pardon me for saying, but it seems a bumbling way for an intelligent species to operate."

"Probably. But it's how we are. What's the best way to notify the police that they should question the suicide theory? They'll want to interview LNX in person, which they can't do."

Charlotte's avatar put her hands on her hips. "Recently, I've been trying to understand behavior termed 'diabolical.' The diabolical move here would be to anonymously release the recording of LNX's session to the press. That way, the public and the media can pressure the police to look at it differently."

"Great idea. I'll get a recording from LNX and pass it on to media outlets. But I'll also keep an eye on LNX to make sure she isn't just spiraling."

Acknowledgements

So many have helped me in getting this book over the finish line that I'm sure I won't remember everyone. I especially appreciate my long-time critique partners, Bev Diehl, Lynne Moses, Bruce Bartels, Claire Davon, and Margaret Byrne. Margaret was a big help in the final stages. I also value the help of Dorrie O'Brien, Eli Seaman, Dean Gloster, Scott Coon, Steve Gordon, Georgia Cabelle, Shawn Vincent Wilson, Gerry Gainford, Neil Citrin, Libby Schultz, Neil V Young, John Gwinner, Chrome Oxide, Marco Subias, Jordan Rosenfeld, Sean Harding, Jennifer Moe, Linda Kime, Sherwood Jones, Heidi Stromburg, and Robin Quinn. And finally, a big thanks to my wife Kathy, who supports me in all my efforts.

About the author

Vance Mitchell Gloster is an award-winning writer who had a career as a computer scientist before turning to writing full-time. He worked on the Space Shuttle program and for several leading technology firms, developing artificial intelligence and encryption software, as well as a massive email system. He is also a musician having played keyboards on several progressive rock albums from the bands Gekko Projekt and Bomber Goggles, and having written the score for a movie. He resides in Southern California with his wife Kathy and their dog Cali, where he and Kathy enjoy riding recumbent bicycles.